Richie left his own personal hell behind when he ran away from his abusive boyfriend, or at least, he'd thought so. But even now that he's back home, he's afraid and can't stop seeing his ex everywhere. He doesn't know if he's strong enough to dig Francis's claws out of him, but he's going to try.

Meeting his mate wasn't part of his plan.

Gilbert's best friend's family has unofficially adopted him. He cares about all seven Long brothers, even Richie, whom he barely knows. Gilbert doesn't understand why he wants to protect Richie and help him heal, but he does, and as long as Richie doesn't push him away, he'll continue.

Richie has no idea how to deal with his mate. His last relationship was a disaster, and he doesn't trust himself anymore. He has to deal with his fears if he wants to be happy, but can he? And as if that weren't bad enough, what will happen when Francis decides to step back into his life?

New Strength
Copyright © 2021 Catherine Lievens
ISBN: 978-1-4874-3372-7
Cover art by Angela Waters

Published by eXtasy Books Inc

Look for us online at:
www.eXtasybooks.com

New Strength
Seven Brothers 5

By

Catherine Lievens

CHAPTER ONE

R ichie stared at the house in front of him. If he'd arrived with his car, he'd have already turned around and left. Since he'd had to hitchhike, there was nowhere for him to go. The only place he could go was forward, which meant walking into the house and facing what was waiting for him.

His family.

He rubbed a hand on his face, instantly regretting it because of the pain. He shouldn't be afraid of his family, and he wasn't, not really. He was afraid of what they'd think of him and of what they'd try to do. They were going to be pissed, and there was nothing he could do about it. He couldn't hide the bruises, unfortunately. He'd left everything behind, including the makeup foundation he used in these situations.

He swallowed. He was always welcome home, but he didn't want to tell anyone what had happened to him, what he'd *allowed* to happen to him. His brothers were strong men, much stronger than he ever could be. How would they look at him?

And he wouldn't be able to hide. They'd have questions, and he didn't know if he could answer them.

He turned away from the house, looking down the street. Even though he was on foot, he could still leave. The problem was that he didn't have money, either. The only things he'd taken with him were his phone and wallet, and even that had been a gamble because Francis might be able to find him through them. He'd turned the phone off, and he didn't know if he would ever turn it back on, but he might need to. He

1

didn't have credit cards to rely on, either.

As a new start, the entire situation was a mess.

It was made worse by the fact that at least some of his brothers were home with their parents. Richie had hoped he'd find his mom and dad alone, but he should have known better. Of seven brothers, he was the only one who didn't live in town and didn't see the rest of the family often. He was the only one who wasn't close to them, and once again, he felt guilty about that.

All of this was his fault. If only he'd been stronger, he wouldn't be in this situation. Unfortunately, he'd been weak, and now he had to deal with the consequences — *all* of the consequences. That included facing his parents and his brothers, having them see he'd been beaten, and having them asking questions.

There was no going back, no matter how much he wished there was.

He sucked in a breath, then another, and, before he could change his mind, he strode to the door. He raised a hand and knocked, still half-hoping no one would be home. He shuffled his feet, looking down the street again. He still had time to run.

But what would he do? Where would he go? He was alone in the world except for his family. Although he'd been without them for a while, he didn't know what he'd do on his own. What he'd allowed to happen was proof he didn't know how to take care of himself. He didn't want his family to take care of him, but he might not have any choice.

How was this any better than the situation left behind?

The door swung open. Richie hadn't known who to expect, but it wasn't his younger brother, Laurie. Laurie tried not to spend too much time with their parents. He was only nineteen and fiercely independent, something Richie admired.

Laurie's eyes went wide. "Richie?"

Richie tried to smile, but that hurt, too. He was pretty sure the smile ended up being more similar to a grimace than anything else. "Hey, baby brother."

There was a guy behind Laurie, but Richie didn't recognize him. His brother usually dated women, so he was surprised, but maybe he shouldn't be. He hadn't talked to Laurie in a while, and his brother had grown up. He'd changed, and Richie hadn't known.

Richie took a step forward to walk into the house. His foot caught on the welcome rug, and he stumbled. Laurie reached for him to keep him on his feet. He grabbed Richie's arm, his hand landing on one of the bruises hidden under Richie's clothes. Richie hissed, but he couldn't do this on his own, so he leaned against his brother, almost crying in relief that someone had him.

Laurie didn't say anything. Instead, he helped Richie into the house. Richie felt like an old man, with all of his body hurting. He wanted nothing more than to go to his childhood bedroom, bury himself under the blankets, and sleep for a week. Maybe by the time he woke up, he'd be able to forget.

"What happened to you?" Laurie asked as he helped Richie sit on a chair in the entrance.

Richie was grateful Laurie wasn't pulling him deeper inside the house for now. The guy was still hovering behind him, reinforcing what Richie thought about him being Laurie's boyfriend. He wished he could distract himself with that, but Laurie wouldn't let it go.

He crouched in front of Richie. "Do I need to get you to a doctor?"

That was the last thing Richie wanted. It was bad enough that his family would find out about everything. He didn't want a stranger to know, too.

He shook his head. "I'll be fine. It's not the first time this has happened." The words were out before he could think

3

better of it. He wanted to suck them back in, but he couldn't.

Laurie frowned. "Who did that to you?"

He was angry, and it soothed something inside Richie. He might not want his brothers to know what had happened, but it felt good to have someone who wanted to protect him and stand up for him. Still, he forced himself to grin. "What will you do if I tell you? Will you go after him and hit him?" If it had been any of Richie's other brothers, Richie would have believed they'd do exactly that. Laurie, though? He didn't talk with his fists.

Laurie leaned back. "No. I can't afford to do that, not with a daughter waiting for me at home. I can send Jack and Andy, though. I'm pretty sure they wouldn't mind doing it for me."

Richie gaped at his brother's words. He'd heard that wrong, hadn't he? There was no way Laurie had just said he had a daughter.

But when Richie looked at the other people stepping into the entrance, his gaze caught on a little girl in Manuel's arms. He recognized Manuel, his brother's mate, but not the baby. Before he could ask who she was, his mother rushed him. She started hugging him, but quickly seemed to think better of it, and instead, she gently touched his shoulders.

"Who's that?" Richie asked, still looking at the baby.

"My daughter, Melissa," Laurie answered. "Are you going to tell us who did this to you?"

Richie shook his head. If he had things his way, he was *never* telling anyone what Francis had done to him. "I promise I'm okay."

"You're not okay," his mom snapped. "That much is obvious, and you're going to tell us what happened."

Richie had heard that tone so many times during his childhood that it almost made him smile. He was home, and no matter how hard the next few weeks would be, how impossible they felt right now, he wasn't alone. He had to remember that. "There's no need for that. I'm moving back home permanently, and that's all you have to know."

Richie had no doubt that eventually his family would find out what happened. Until then, he'd do his best to hide everything from them. He didn't want them to look at him with pity — or worse, disgust — because he hadn't been able to defend himself.

"When did you move away?" Laurie asked.

Richie had never told his family he was moving out of town. Francis hadn't given him time, and since Richie barely saw his parents and his brothers anyway, he hadn't wanted to make waves. "I should have told you," he said to no one in particular. "I left town a few months ago, and it was the worst thing I could have done. That's over, though." He was never going back. He couldn't.

"Does it have to do with Francis?" Jack asked.

Richie glared at his brother. He'd tried keeping his relationship from his family, but with six brothers, it was never easy.

"Who's this Francis?" Manuel asked.

"Richie's boyfriend. Was he the one who hit you?"

Damn Jack. He'd always seen too much, even though usually he behaved like he didn't have a care in the world.

Richie didn't want to have this conversation, so he tried getting to his feet. He should have known his mother wouldn't allow that to happen. She pushed him back into the chair, and he glared at her, too. Since there was no way he was talking back at her, he turned his attention to Jack.

"Don't stick your nose into this. Whatever happened with Francis is over. He's never going to touch me again, and I want you to leave him alone."

Because the last thing Richie wanted was for his family to get hurt because of him, which was what would happen if they contacted Francis. No, it was better for all of them to stay away from Francis. Hopefully, he wouldn't come looking for Richie.

But Richie wasn't betting on that.

Gilbert had peeked into the entrance when everyone had rushed there, but he'd quickly retreated when he'd seen what was happening.

He knew Richie, although not personally. Laurie always talked about his brothers, but Richie was the one he mentioned least often. Apparently, Richie had always kept to himself, which Gilbert could understand. Having six brothers couldn't be easy. There seemed to have been something more behind it, but it was none of Gilbert's business. It wasn't his place to stick his nose in this situation, so he'd retreated to the kitchen.

He'd started cleaning up, unable to stop thinking about what was happening in the entrance. He'd known Laurie for a few years, and Laurie was his best friend. Gilbert had been surprised to get so close to him, but he loved him. He also loved Laurie's family, and he was closer to them than he was to his own father. He knew all the brothers except for Richie.

Gilbert frowned. He really should have met Richie before, since he'd been coming around for a few years. Why hadn't he? He couldn't remember ever seeing Richie before except in passing, and as far as he could remember, Richie had never come to a family dinner. Gilbert tried to be there every time he could, even though the Longs weren't his family.

He had so many questions, but he wouldn't get answers to any of them. He had to stay away from the family for now, and he didn't mind cleaning up. That way, Marie would be able to focus on her son.

Gilbert had heard enough of the conversation to realize something was very wrong. The brothers had looked like they were ready to leave the house and find whoever had hurt their brother, and even though Gilbert was an only child, he understood the feeling. He'd hurt anyone who dared to beat Laurie the way Richie had been beaten.

Gilbert winced when he thought about the wounds. They were the things he'd noticed right away. How could he not? Richie's lower lip was split open, and while there was no blood to be seen, it had to be painful. That wasn't the worst of it, though. Richie's left eye was so swollen it would be a miracle if he could see anything through it. A large bruise covered part of his jaw, disappearing into the collar of his shirt, a sure sign there were more of them hidden under there. The way Richie moved also confirmed that. Gilbert suspected that every movement hurt him, and he was surprised to realize he wanted to go to Richie, get him into bed, and take care of him.

Someone had beaten Richie up, and from what little Gilbert had heard before leaving the room, everyone knew who that someone was.

"What are you doing?" Marie asked as she walked into the kitchen. Her eyes were red, but she wasn't crying.

"I'm cleaning up. I figured you had better things to focus on."

She grabbed one of the plates Gilbert had already rinsed and rinsed it again. "I can do that. You should go to the others."

"I'm sure they'd rather have some family time."

"You're family, and you belong with us."

It wasn't the first time Marie said something like that, but Gilbert suspected that he should stay away in this situation. Still, he was worried. "How's Richie?"

Marie put down the plate she was still holding. "I don't know. Have you seen him?"

"I have." That was why Gilbert was asking.

Marie's expression crumpled, and Gilbert wondered if she

was going to cry. She rubbed her eyes, her shoulders slumping. "He won't tell us what happened to him, but I think Jack knows something. I wanted to ask him, but not in front of Richie. He's already been hurt enough."

And if Richie didn't want his mother to know what happened to him, he should be allowed to keep it to himself. Gilbert doubted he would. The family didn't have secrets, at least not secrets that lasted. They always found out if something happened to one of theirs.

"I'm sure he'll tell you when he feels ready," Gilbert murmured.

Marie nodded and smiled, but it was tremulous. "We should give him time."

Gilbert wrapped his arms around Marie and pulled her into a hug. She wasn't his mother, but she'd welcomed him with open arms, and he would never forget that. It was thanks to her and the rest of her family that he would always have a safe place. "I'm sure he'll be fine."

She gently pushed him away. "Of course he will. He has us, and he's home. Why don't you go to the others? I'll finish cleaning up."

Gilbert wanted to say no, but how could he? Maybe he'd manage to sneak away without anyone noticing. He suspected they were all too focused on Richie anyway.

But when he went to the living room to grab his things, he found Laurie pacing the floor, Melissa in his arms. Richard and Alexis had moved to the living room, too, as had Richie, who was sitting on the edge of the couch, looking like he wanted to run away. Jack was leaning against the wall, a scowl on his face.

Richie probably did want to run. As much as Gilbert loved this family, they could be a lot. Not everyone was here today, which was a relief, but he had no doubt they'd be informed about what had happened soon. He's give it half an hour before all the brothers and their mates were home to talk to Richie.

"Why won't you tell us what happened?" Laurie asked. He squeezed Melissa, who giggled and grabbed a lock of his hair. Laurie reached up and untangled her fingers.

"Because it's none of your business," Richie said.

He sounded wary and tired, like he wanted nothing more than to get into bed. That was probably the case, but Gilbert didn't suggest he do it.

Laurie stopped in front of his brother. "How can you say that? Have you looked at yourself in the mirror today?"

"Laurie," Laurie's father warned.

He was always the voice of reason in the family, one of the calmer elements. From what Gilbert had seen, the only son who'd taken after him when it came to that was Hugh, who was usually quiet. The rest of his brothers, not so much. Gilbert didn't know how Richie was, but for now, he wasn't a talker.

"What?" Laurie asked. "How can you be so calm?"

"It's Richie's decision if he doesn't want to tell us what happened to him or who did this," Richard slowly said. His eyes were blazing, though, which told Gilbert he wasn't as calm as he was trying to act.

Gilbert wondered if he should just sneak out and come back for his cell phone later. He would have done just that if his car keys hadn't been with it. As it was, he had no way to go home, which meant he was stuck, even though it made him uncomfortable.

"At least tell us where Francis is," Jack said.

"I'm not going to do that," Richie said.

"Why not?"

"Because I'm not an idiot. You'd go find him, and I don't want that to happen."

"He hurt you," Jack said. His voice was softer now but no

gentler. He sounded like if he got his hands on Francis, Francis wouldn't see tomorrow.

Gilbert tended to agree with that. The problem was that no one here knew if Francis actually was responsible for this. Richie had hinted at it, but he hadn't been open, and Gilbert understood. He might not have brothers, but he'd been spending enough time with Laurie's to know what they'd do if they knew where this Francis guy was. They'd hunt him down and make sure he could never hurt Richie again. That was why Richie wasn't telling them where he was, and it was smart.

Gilbert might not know what had happened, but even he could tell that having the brothers find Francis and beat him up would only make things worse.

Richie had no intention of telling anyone where Francis was. He could too easily imagine what his brothers would do, and while he didn't care what happened to Francis, Francis wouldn't take whatever Richie's brothers rained upon him nicely. If he couldn't hurt them, he'd try to hurt Richie, and he'd already done enough of that. Richie didn't want to go through it again.

Besides, he wanted to forget Francis had ever existed. He didn't want to think about him ever again, and telling his family what had happened meant he'd have to talk about him.

He swallowed and looked around. Since he didn't want to talk about Francis, it was better to distract everyone. Thankfully, it should be fairly easy because Richie had questions. "When did you become a dad?" he asked Laurie.

Laurie's eyes narrowed. "Don't think I don't know what you're doing," he said.

Richie tried to look innocent, but from the way Laurie grimaced, he didn't think he'd managed. "I'm curious. You're only nineteen, and you were always going around saying that you weren't going to settle down anytime soon, yet, it looks like you did." Melissa's mom was nowhere to be seen, and Richie was curious about that, too.

Laurie huffed and sat next to Richie on the couch. "Trust me. I wasn't planning on settling down. I also wasn't planning on having children so young. I know I messed up, and I don't need you to remind me of that, too."

Richie raised his hands. "I'm not going to say anything about that since I don't know the situation."

Melissa peered at him. She didn't seem to be afraid, but she looked fascinated, maybe with Richie's injuries. Richie offered her a finger, which she swiftly took. She tried to stuff it into her mouth right away, so Richie had to pull it away from her.

Laurie sighed. "I dated her mother for a few weeks. She didn't tell me she was pregnant, just appeared on my doorstep one day, handed me Melissa, and told me she had a work interview and that I had to take care of the baby."

Richie gaped. "That's how you learned you had a daughter?"

"I did. I made sure Candace knew what I thought about that, but it doesn't change the fact that Melissa is my daughter." He cleared his throat. "And that I found my mate."

Richie had no idea what to say. He looked at the guy who'd been hovering by Laurie since Richie had arrived. "Which I suppose is him."

Richie had always expected Laurie's mate to be a woman. He realized now that it was because as far as he knew, Laurie had only dated women. Richie had never asked Laurie if he was straight or something else, and maybe he should have. He *would* have if he hadn't been dealing with Francis and trying to survive.

He was a shitty older brother, wasn't he? Laurie had been

through so much, but Richie hadn't been there with him. He hadn't been alone since he'd had their brothers, but still. Richie should have been there for him.

Laurie nodded. "This is Alexis, my mate," he confirmed. He looked up at Alexis, adoration clear in his gaze.

Richie had to look away. It reminded him too much of Francis, who had looked at him the same way in the beginning. He'd eventually realized it was all a show, but it wasn't a show for Laurie. He truly cared for his mate.

"I'm happy you found him," Richie said. He smiled at Alexis, who smiled back. He looked wary, but then Richie supposed it made sense. Alexis didn't know him. Since Richie was refusing to explain what happened to him, there was a chance Laurie and Melissa could get hurt.

Not that Francis would do anything like that. The only person he'd ever hurt was Richie, and he wouldn't dare touch a baby. Still, Richie wondered if he'd done the wrong thing coming here. He wouldn't have if he'd had anywhere else to go.

Richie's father gently squeezed his shoulder. "I'm going to find your mom. Will you be okay?"

Richie nodded. He was more okay than he'd been recently, even though his entire body hurt.

"I have to make a phone call," Jack declared.

He left the room without looking back, and Richie knew his brother would be trouble. He'd have to keep an eye on him, but he wasn't sure how when he couldn't even get up from the couch now that he was on it.

The room slowly emptied until only Richie, Laurie, and Melissa were left. At least, that was what Richie thought until he looked up and made eye contact with a guy that he vaguely remembered but couldn't quite place.

"That's Gilbert," Laurie said. "My best friend."

Richie blinked. "Since when? Wasn't your best friend

named Bryson?"

Laurie rolled his eyes. "When I was in high school. I met Gilbert a few years ago, and I'm closer to him than I've ever been to anyone, including Bryson."

So Laurie and Gilbert had been best friends for at least a few years. How could Richie not know about this? But then, he'd met Francis three years ago. He supposed he'd been focused on other things. Still, he was surprised he hadn't taken more notice, because Gilbert was cute.

His hair was dark blond and cut short, although not so short that someone wouldn't be able to bury their fingers there, maybe while kissing him. His green eyes looked worried, and Richie wasn't sure why. It wasn't like Gilbert knew him. He was a bit shorter than Richie, but his legs were long under his tight jeans.

"I should go," Gilbert said.

He'd clearly been at this family dinner, which meant Richie's parents considered him a part of the family. Richie didn't want to push him to leave, but he also didn't want a stranger to watch him. Of course, it was too late for that.

"Why?" Laurie asked. "Come here. You know Melissa will start crying if you leave."

Gilbert rolled his eyes, but he moved closer. He sat in the armchair next to the couch, and now, he was close enough that Richie could see the freckles on his nose. They spread down, peppering his upper lip and making him even more kissable than he'd been before.

Richie blinked at his thoughts. Was he really thinking about kissing Gilbert?

He hadn't thought he'd want to kiss anyone for years, not after what the last man he'd kissed had done to him. He wasn't interested in Gilbert. He couldn't be.

"Don't use your daughter to keep me here," Gilbert said.

"I'm not. You know she loves her uncle Gilbert." He looked

down at his daughter. "You want to go to your uncle, right?"

"You should just be honest and say you want to go make out with Alexis," Gilbert said.

"Me? I'd never do something like that. You know how uncomfortable Alexis is about doing that kind of thing here."

Richie snickered. He could understand where Alexis was coming from. With so many brothers around, there was always someone walking in on you.

Gilbert leaned forward to take Melissa while still teasing Laurie. Melissa seemed more than happy to go into his arms, and she reached for him. Laurie had to pass her in front of Richie's face so Gilbert could catch her, which brought both him and Gilbert close to Richie.

He couldn't avoid Gilbert's scent hitting him in the face. He couldn't avoid realizing there was a good reason he was fascinated by Gilbert.

He couldn't avoid freaking out when he realized that Gilbert was his mate.

Gilbert had been wary of moving so close to Richie because he didn't want to spook him. He knew he had when Richie's expression contorted and he leaned back as far as he could against the couch. His eyes were wide, and he'd paled as if he'd seen a ghost.

Gilbert quickly grabbed Melissa and brought her against his chest. She cooed and started sucking on her fingers. Gilbert's attention was on Richie, though.

"I'm sorry. I didn't mean to crowd you."

Richie shook his head. His hair was too long, and it fell in front of his eyes. Richie had to tuck it behind his ears, and he did so while not looking at Gilbert. "I'm fine."

He sounded and looked nowhere near fine, but Gilbert knew better than to push. He might not know for sure what had happened to Richie, but he could put things together. Richie had left his boyfriend and had all but admitted the guy had been beating him. He'd been abused, and while Gilbert wanted nothing more than to go after his ex, he stayed where he was. He'd have to wait for Richie's brothers to get to the guy. They'd take care of him when the time came.

"Are you—you're human?" Richie asked.

Gilbert hadn't expected the conversation to go that way, but it wasn't a bad thing. It was better to distract Richie from his situation. "I am."

Richie's shoulders slumped as if he were relieved. Was his ex-boyfriend a shifter? Had the guy taken advantage of that to hurt Richie? Gilbert's rage when he thought of that didn't make sense, but he supposed it was because he considered Richie to be family. They weren't related by blood, but Gilbert had always felt welcome here. He wanted to protect Richie because Richie's family had protected him.

Of course, it was nowhere near the same thing. Gilbert hadn't been abused by anyone, even though his father was an asshole. But Richie was going to need a lot of care and love, and there was no one better than his family to give him that.

Melissa slapped a damp hand against Gilbert's cheek. He chuckled and pushed her hand away before rubbing his cheek with his palm. "When do babies stop putting everything in their mouth?" he asked.

"I actually looked it up," Laurie whined. "It's going to take years before she stops doing it."

Gilbert grimaced. He loved Melissa, but he could do without her slobbering all over the place.

Laurie's father walked back into the living room. His gaze went straight to Richie, but he relaxed when he saw that Richie was still sitting there on the couch.

Gilbert sighed. The family needed time and space to deal with this, and even though he was closer to them than he'd ever been to his own father, this wasn't his place.

He got to his feet and handed Melissa back to Laurie. "I should go."

"Why?" Laurie asked, getting up, too. "We haven't had dessert yet."

"It's fine. I have something to do anyway."

Laurie's eyes narrowed, and Gilbert knew his best friend didn't believe him. He was right, because Gilbert had nothing to do except go back to his apartment and spend the rest of the evening on his own on his couch. He felt like he was intruding, though, and while he might have stayed if any of the other brothers had been in trouble, he didn't think he should with Richie. He and Richie didn't know each other, so for Richie, Gilbert was an intruder. Hopefully, in time, he'd accept Gilbert into his and his family's life. For now, Gilbert believed it was better for everyone if he left.

"Mom isn't going to be happy if you leave without saying goodbye," North said.

Gilbert glared at him. "I know what you're doing."

"Me? I'm not doing anything."

But he was. They both knew Marie would try to stop Gilbert from going just yet. She mothered him as if he were one of her sons, and Gilbert would have given in any other day. He couldn't do that to Richie, though. "I'll go say goodbye."

He waved at Richard, but the man was focused on his son and barely looked at him. Gilbert wasn't offended. He snatched his phone and his car keys from the table he'd left them on and headed toward the kitchen. He could hear Jack talking somewhere in the house, and he didn't sound happy. Gilbert wouldn't want to be Francis when the brothers managed to get their hands on the guy.

Marie was still in the kitchen, making coffee. She appeared better when she looked up, although her eyes were still red. She frowned when she saw he was holding his car keys.

"Where are you going? We're not done eating yet."

"I have something to do. I'm sorry, but I forgot about it until now."

Marie stared at Gilbert. He knew she didn't believe him, but he wasn't sure whether or not she'd call him out on it. He was relieved when she didn't. Instead, she stepped closer and hugged him.

"You're a good boy," she told him.

Gilbert would have been offended if anyone else had called him a boy. He was twenty, not a kid. But Marie saw all her sons as her boys, and it made him feel like one of them when she called him that.

He hugged her back. It was as much for her as for him, and when they stepped away from each other, he could see she was more relaxed.

"Thank you," he told her.

"You're welcome to come over for dinner anytime, even if Laurie isn't there."

Marie had been telling Gilbert that since the day they'd met, but Gilbert had never dared accept the offer. Maybe he should, one of these days. "I'll come," he confirmed. "Although I'm sure you have other things to focus on other than me right now."

"I just want all my babies to be safe. I hate to see him that way."

"He'll heal." At least physically. It would be harder to heal mentally, but Richie wasn't alone. His entire family was ready to stand behind him and help him any way they could, and while the brothers might not understand how important that was, Gilbert did.

He still had family on his mind when he left the house and walked to his car. He knew he shouldn't, but he found himself taking his phone out once he was in the car. He stared at the screen, wondering what his father would do if he called.

There was only one way for him to find out, wasn't there?

Gilbert dialed the number and waited for his father to answer. He thought the man wouldn't and was about to hang up when his father's voice reached him.

"Hello?"

"Hi. It's me, Gilbert."

The silence that greeted Gilbert's words was long enough to turn awkward. "Gilbert. Was there something you needed?"

"No. I just thought we could talk."

"I can't right now."

Gilbert sighed. He should have known better than to hope. What had he thought would happen? That his father would apologize? The man was convinced he was right, and nothing would budge that conviction. "All right. I'm sorry I bothered you."

But his father had already hung up. Gilbert lowered the phone and stared at the screen for a moment before shaking his head and throwing the phone in the passenger seat. Until his father accepted that Gilbert was gay, there would be no reconciliation between them. Gilbert had to wrap his mind around that and accept it.

He was sad, but he had to remember he wasn't alone. The Longs didn't care that he was gay, and they never had. How could they, when none of the seven brothers was straight? But Gilbert knew that even if they had been, the Longs would have accepted him. It was just the way they were and the way he wished his father was.

CHAPTER TWO

R ichie rinsed his hair, closing his eyes. The water was warm against his skin, comforting and reassuring.

He'd been staying with his parents for the past few days. The bruises were already fading, and while his eye was still swollen, it was healing, too. He hoped that soon every sign that he'd been beaten up would be gone so he could go out and find a job without people staring at him, asking him what had happened, or worse, deciding they didn't want to hire him because of how he looked. He couldn't wait to find a job and earn money, although it would take him a while to have enough to buy a car and find an apartment.

He realized he was lucky that his parents didn't have a problem with him staying with them. If he didn't have them, he'd be on the streets, and it was too easy to imagine how bad that would be. Instead, he had a roof over his head, a warm bed, and food. A lot of people wouldn't understand why he wanted to leave as soon as possible, but they hadn't grown up with six brothers.

The bathroom door slammed open, making him jump. His feet slipped on the wet tub, and he scrambled to grab something, *anything*, that would keep him from falling on his face. The last thing he needed was to get hurt again or to break something.

A hand shot behind the shower curtain and grabbed his arm. He was grateful for it, but he still shook it off as soon as he was steady on his feet. He grabbed the curtain and wrapped it around his body before peeking out.

"What are you doing in the bathroom?" he asked Andy.

"I have to use the toilet."

Richie was going to kill someone, and that someone would be one of his brothers. He was sure of it. "Couldn't you wait until I was done?"

"Why? I don't have anything you haven't already seen."

That much was true. There was no way to grow up with six brothers without seeing all of them in various states of undress over the years. The house only had three bathrooms, after all. "The fact that I've already seen it doesn't mean I want to see it again. Go away and come back when I'm done."

Andy pouted. "But I have to go."

"Then use Mom and Dad's bathroom."

"You know Mom doesn't want us to use her bathroom."

"Maybe because you don't clean up after yourself? Go away."

Andy stomped his way out of the bathroom. He slammed the door behind himself, but Richie still waited for a few minutes before stepping away from the curtain and letting it go. He sighed heavily and tilted his head under the water spray to finish rinsing.

He loved his family, but gosh, they could be annoying sometimes.

It was one of the reasons he wanted to leave. As grateful as he was to his parents for welcoming him home when he needed it, his brothers were around too much. He hadn't realized that would be the case, maybe because he hadn't been home in at least a year, if not more. He couldn't remember.

Francis had never liked Richie visiting his family, and while he'd allowed it for the first two years they'd been together, he hadn't after that. If Richie wanted to see his brothers, he had to do it on the sly, and coming home was the furthest thing from that. Francis hadn't allowed Richie to come to their family dinners or be around his parents in general, which was why Richie had been surprised to find out his brothers regularly came and went from the house. They were as welcome here as he was, which was good — except when he needed to shower.

He finished rinsing and stepped out of the tub, grabbed his towel, and quickly dried off. He kept an eye on the door, wondering if Andy would burst through again, but he didn't. In hindsight, Richie should have locked the door, but he hadn't seen a reason to. The other times he'd showered, no one had been home except his parents, and they seemed more than happy to give him space.

That wouldn't last. Eventually, both Richie's parents and his brothers would corner him and demand an explanation. They'd been more patient than Richie had expected, and while he was grateful for the respite, he was also wary of it ending. He didn't want to tell them what he'd allowed Francis to do to him. He didn't want them to realize he'd been so weak he'd stayed with Francis even after his boyfriend had started beating him.

Richie needed to do something, but what? He didn't want to push his family away again. He'd just gotten them back. He might need his space, but it didn't mean he didn't love his family. They were boisterous, noisy, invasive, and a lot to deal with on the best of days, but he'd been used to it once. Surely he could get used to it again.

Besides, no matter how much he didn't to tell them what happened, no matter how much he wished he had more privacy, he felt safe here. Francis knew where the house was, which was one of the reasons Richie wanted to leave as soon as possible, but Richie was never alone. If Francis came here, he wouldn't just find Richie.

Of course, that possibility also terrified Richie. What if he was home alone with his mother or his father and Francis arrived? As far as he knew, Francis had never hurt anyone but

Richie but there was a first time for anything, and besides, Richie didn't know Francis as well as he'd thought he did. He wouldn't put it past him to hurt Richie's mother or his father, and that was one thing Richie couldn't allow him to do.

Francis was still calling and texting. Richie had given in and turned on his phone again, and when he had, he'd received no less than sixty-three messages. Francis had also called him more than fifty times, and while Richie had been overwhelmed, he had no intention of calling him back. He hadn't been able to avoid reading the messages, though, and the thought of them still made him sick to his stomach.

He swallowed and grabbed his clothes, needing to get dressed as soon as possible.

Those texts still invaded his mind. They'd started innocently enough, with Francis asking him where he was, then telling him he was getting worried. Those texts had made Richie snort. Francis wasn't worried something had happened to him. He was concerned Richie would tell someone what he'd done to him, nothing more.

Then Francis had started to apologize. He always did that after he got violent, and Richie had stopped believing he was sorry a long time ago. It didn't matter how many times Francis told him he hadn't meant to do it. Richie knew he had, and he couldn't fool himself that wasn't the case.

His mouth tasted bitter from the memories. Every time Francis had said he hadn't meant to hurt him, he'd also added that it was Richie's fault. It was because Richie hadn't worn the clothes Francis wanted him to wear, or maybe because he'd overcooked the roast for dinner. Francis didn't need a reason to start beating Richie.

After the apologies, the threatening texts had started. Francis had written that he'd make Richie pay if he told anyone what happened. When Richie hadn't answered those, either, Francis had started threatening Richie's family. He'd said that if they tried anything against him, he'd make sure they and Richie paid for it.

That was one of the reasons Richie couldn't tell anyone about Francis. He'd already said too much, and between that and what his family knew, they suspected what had happened. It was bad enough without giving them details.

Richie couldn't allow Francis to hurt his family. They were everything he had left in the world.

Except for his mate.

Richie huffed out a breath and leaned against the sink. He couldn't believe any of this. He was on the run from his abusive ex-boyfriend who didn't realize he was an ex, and here he was, meeting his mate. What was he supposed to do with all of this? He was nowhere near ready or willing to have another relationship, even with his mate. Gilbert seemed like a nice enough guy, but then, so had Francis when Richie had first met him. How was Richie supposed to trust someone new? How was he supposed to let go of the pain and fear to give Gilbert a chance?

Richie wasn't sure he could, and that was one more thing Francis had taken from him. He'd never forgive him for this and for everything else. He'd have to work harder to forget it, though. If he wanted a chance at a normal life, maybe with Gilbert, he had to let go of Francis. But how was he supposed to do that when Francis wasn't letting go of him?

Once again, Gilbert was headed to the Longs' house. He felt like he was spending more time there than at his own apartment these days, and he wasn't sure why. Sure, he enjoyed spending time with Marie and Richard, and he had before, too, but something had changed recently, and the only thing he could think of was Richie.

Gilbert liked him. They hadn't exactly talked a lot, but he'd seen Richie a few times since he'd arrived. He'd relaxed, which made Gilbert happy. He wanted Richie to stop being afraid, but it would take time. Still, seeing him at home with his family was good, and Gilbert hoped Richie knew everyone would be there for him if he needed them. They'd been there for Gilbert, and he wasn't even related to them.

He wasn't going to the house for dinner today, though. Marie had cooked him a casserole, and she wanted him to pick it up. He'd told her she didn't need to feed him and that he was more than able to cook for himself, but her only answer had been to glare at him. She fed all her boys, and Gilbert was one of them now.

It was strange and not easy to get used to. Gilbert had lost his mother when he was thirteen, and his father had never been a warm parent. He'd given Gilbert what he needed when it came to food and clothes, but that was about it. He'd certainly never cared about Gilbert the way Marie did. He also wasn't falling all over himself to make sure Gilbert had food ready in his fridge so he wouldn't have to cook when he came home too tired to do so. Marie didn't want Gilbert or her sons to get too much takeout, which was why she cooked for all of them at least twice a week. One of those times, they went over and ate with her and her husband. The other, they picked up the food she'd cooked and took it home.

Gilbert had never felt like he was part of his family the way he did with the Longs.

His phone vibrated where he'd left it on the passenger seat, and he quickly looked at it. He was surprised to see his father was calling. He looked around, found a parking lot, and turned so he could answer the phone call. His mouth was dry when he did so. Had his father finally come to accept that Gilbert was gay? Was he calling to apologize?

Gilbert had come out to him when he was eighteen. He hadn't dared sooner because his father had taken the death of

Gilbert's mother hard. So had Gilbert, but he'd been able to get himself out and grieve more easily than his father. He'd thought his father wouldn't care, but instead, he'd exploded. He'd blamed himself for Gilbert being gay, as if by being a widowed father, he'd caused it.

"Hello?" Gilbert answered. He didn't even care if his father wasn't ready to apologize. He just wanted to talk to him, to explain that the way he'd been raised had nothing to do with his sexuality. He didn't know if his father would believe it, but if he had the opportunity, he'd try anyway.

"Gilbert."

"How are you?"

Gilbert's father grunted. "I'm fine. I was looking for your mother's recipe book."

Gilbert's stomach turned to lead. His father hadn't called to apologize or even to talk to him. He wanted something from him, nothing more.

It was hard to swallow, but Gilbert forced himself to. "I have it."

"You stole it?"

Gilbert's father sounded angry, but so was Gilbert. "I didn't steal it. She told me she wanted me to have it. Besides, you only now realized it was gone. How did it take you seven years?"

Gilbert knew the answer to that. His father didn't cook. He'd made sure Gilbert had food growing up, but it was all things that only had to be stuck in the microwave or takeout. That was probably one of the reasons Marie mothered Gilbert so much.

"You had no right to take it," Gilbert's father snapped. "I need you to give it back."

"Why? Are you going to start cooking?" Because if he wasn't, he didn't have a need for the recipe book Gilbert cherished.

25

He and his mother had cooked together when he was a kid. They'd stopped when he was twelve, but then he'd been growing up, and his mother had gotten sick. He wished he could go back in time and cook with her again, but using her recipe book was the next best thing.

"Lucy said something about wanting it, and I agreed to give it to her," Gilbert's father said.

Gilbert didn't know what to say to that. It wasn't that he didn't want his cousin to use those recipes, but why would his father give the book to her? "Why?"

"Because she asked for it, and she's a woman."

"And since I'm a guy, I shouldn't cook, right?" Gilbert's father didn't answer, but Gilbert knew what he thought.

It was ridiculous. His father wasn't eighty, for fuck's sake. Why did he insist on holding onto the traditional female and male roles? He realized his parents had. His mother had stayed home after she'd gotten pregnant with him, and she'd never gone back to work. His father had been the one to earn money while she took care of the house and Gilbert. After she died, there had been no one to cook for them and no one to clean. Gilbert had done what he could, but his father had never liked him cleaning. Gilbert hadn't wanted to live in a pigsty, which was why he'd started doing it in secret.

He'd been relieved when he'd been able to move out. Having his own apartment meant a lot, even though it sucked financially.

"I just want the book. I promised Lucy I'd give it to her."

"Well, you're going to have to tell Lucy you changed your mind. I'm not giving it back. Mom wanted *me* to have it, not Lucy."

"Don't be an idiot. I already promised."

"Then tell her you don't know where it is!" Gilbert sucked in a breath. He'd been hopeful when he'd seen his father was calling, but he shouldn't have been. Still, he hadn't expected this.

How could his father do this to him? Didn't he understand how important the book was to Gilbert? Even though Gilbert wasn't cooking much lately, he still cherished it. His mother had written all the recipes by hand, adding little notes and even pictures of the dishes she and Gilbert had created when he was young. It wouldn't matter even if Gilbert had never cooked one dish out of it.

He had many memories of his mother and many mementos, but this was the most important to him. He loved his cousin, but he wasn't handing it over. Besides, he doubted Lucy knew about this. She'd probably mentioned the book and that she wanted to cook stuff out of it, and Gilbert's father had agreed to give it to her because he didn't have a need for it. Lucy would be horrified when she found out.

"Stop acting like an idiot," Gilbert's father said.

Gilbert was done with this phone call. "And stop being heartless. Sometimes, I don't understand how Mom could have fallen in love with you. You're an asshole."

Gilbert didn't wait for his father to answer. He hung up and threw his phone on the passenger seat, needing it to be away from him so he wouldn't chuck it out the window. He couldn't afford to replace the damn thing.

Gilbert needed to stop worrying about his father and what the man thought of him. Yes, he was sad that his father couldn't accept him for who he was and was a heartless asshole, but being sad wouldn't change the man. Only he could change himself, and that wouldn't happen until he wanted to.

Gilbert wasn't a good enough reason for him to do that, and he had to accept that and finally allow himself to move on.

"We'd like you to come downstairs to talk," Richie's mother

said through the door.

After his shower, Richie had retreated to his bedroom. He knew Andy was still in the house, and from the sound of it, he wasn't alone. Since the brother he was closer to was Jack, Richie would bet Jack was there, too. The last thing Richie wanted was to talk to his brothers. He didn't even want to talk to his parents, but he felt he owed them this conversation. He wasn't sure how much he'd tell them, but he couldn't keep on hiding without them worrying, and he didn't want them to.

"I'll only talk to the two of you," he said.

"Jack and Andy would like to be there, too."

Richie snorted. "If they had their way, all of my brothers would be there. I don't want to do this in front of them." Because while Richie wouldn't like his parents knowing how weak he was, he absolutely loathed having to tell his brothers.

He was right in the middle when it came to age. Hugh and Sean, along with Curtis, were older than him. Jack, Andy, and Laurie were younger. Richie might be able to reason with the older three when it came to this situation, but he doubted he'd be able to convince Jack not to go find Francis and beat him up. Laurie wouldn't because of Melissa, while Richie wasn't sure about Andy. About Jack, he was, and he didn't want his brother to get hurt.

"All right. I'll tell them to go. Will you talk to your father and me, though?"

Richie wanted to say no, but instead, he agreed. "I will."

He listened to his mother's footsteps fade. Then he listened some more. He wasn't surprised when he heard Jack's voice protesting. He loved his brother, and he was grateful that Jack wanted to be there for him, but he didn't need him to fight his battles.

Or maybe he did. He clearly needed protecting, since he hadn't been able to stand up to Francis. He didn't want his brother to have to do it, though. He wanted to become strong enough to stand up to Francis without help.

"That's bullshit!" Jack yelled. "Richie? Get your ass down here. I want to talk to you."

Richie knew his brother wouldn't hurt him. None of them would. Still, he didn't like when people got angry, so he stayed right where he was, hiding behind his bedroom door. He couldn't make out what Jack was saying. He could tell someone was telling him to let go and leave, and Jack wasn't happy about that.

"Fine," Jack yelled. "I'm going for now. This isn't over, though. I'll find out what happened to you even if it's the last thing I do, and I'll find that asshole, too. That's a promise I'm making you, Richie."

After a moment, the front door slammed, making Richie jump and grimace. He knew better than not to take Jack seriously. He might be younger than Richie and only twenty-five, but he was fiercely protective of all the brothers, including the ones older than him. He wouldn't let this go, which meant Richie would have to find a way to talk to him without making him angry enough that he'd go after Francis.

"Richie? They're gone," Richie's mother said.

Richie sucked in a breath and got to his feet. He left his bedroom, relieved his mother hadn't come upstairs to get him. He knew where he'd find both her and his father. Their family always had their essential conversations in the kitchen.

Sure enough, they were sitting at the counter when he got there. Instead of sitting with them, he went to the fridge and grabbed a bottle of water. He hung onto it as he leaned against the counter.

He didn't want to look at his parents, but he felt he owed them at least a few answers. The fact that his phone was vibrating in his pocket didn't help, though. He should have turned it off and ignored it, but he wanted to know what Francis was up to. He had no doubt that eventually his ex-boyfriend would come to the house, and he wanted to know when that would happen if possible.

"Are you ready to talk?" Richie's mother asked.

Richie shook his head. "I don't see what there is to talk about. Yes, someone beat me up. I left, though, and I'm not going back. Isn't that enough for you?"

"It could be," Richie's father said slowly. "But I'm worried about who beat you up. From what Jack said, he thinks it was your boyfriend. Is he right?"

Richie closed his eyes. "He is. I don't know if you remember Francis." Richie had met him three years ago, but Francis had never cared about Richie's family. In the beginning, he'd found excuses not to meet them. Only later had Richie realized it was because he didn't *want* to meet them. It was easy to imagine what Richie's family would have done if they'd realized what Francis was doing to him. Francis probably knew that, too.

Francis also hadn't wanted Richie to have a support system. Richie had never lost his family, but he'd put distance between them, so much so that he hadn't been sure they'd welcome him home. Between that and not wanting them to realize how weak he was, it had taken Richie way too long to get away from Francis.

All of that was in the past now. Richie wanted to move forward, and he didn't think he'd be able to if he didn't tell his family at least part of what happened. Besides, he wanted his parents and his brothers to know to be careful around Francis. He doubted Francis would hurt any of them, but he might come around and ask about Richie, and if they didn't know, they might tell him where Richie was. Richie didn't plan to stay with his parents forever, and once he found an apartment, they'd know the address. The worst thing that could happen would be if they told Francis where it was.

"Only vaguely," Richie's mother said. "I remember you

talked about him a few times. We never met him, though."

"That's because he didn't want to meet you. He also didn't want me to have contact with you, which is why I slowly withdrew. I'm sorry I did that. I shouldn't have."

"It doesn't matter. We just want you to be safe."

"And that's the only reason I'm telling you about this. Francis isn't an easy man to be with." There was no way Richie was telling his parents about all of the abuse, but he had to share something. "Sometimes, he becomes violent. He's the one who beat me up."

There was a moment of silence before his father asked, "It wasn't the first time it happened, was it?"

Richie's mouth tasted like ash. He took a sip of water, but it didn't help. "It wasn't," he confirmed. "But it's over. I got away from him, and I'm home."

"And that's all that matters," Richie's mother said. "We want you to be safe and happy. Do you think Francis is going to come after you?"

"It's a possibility. If you see him, don't tell him where I am."

"Of course not."

"And please, don't start a fight with him. I don't want either of you or my brothers to get hurt. I don't need you to get revenge for me or anything like that. I know that the past three years have been a mess, but I got out. I only want to focus on the future and to leave Francis behind."

"I'm not sure your brothers will agree to that. You heard Jack."

Richie grimaced. "I did, but I need him to stay away from Francis. I just want to forget Francis was ever in my life, please."

"I'll talk to him," Richie's father said gruffly. "But none of them will be happy about it."

"I don't need them to be happy about it. I just need them

to respect what I want and do it."

Richie's life was already complicated enough without having one or more of his brothers hunt Francis down and hurt him.

Richie's mother got to her feet. He tensed when she walked around the counter, but his mother would never hurt him. Still, he couldn't help but cringe when she reached for him. She paused, then wrapped her arms around him, pulling him into her arms. Richie only stayed tense for a moment. Then he hugged his mother back and buried his face against her neck. He took a deep breath, inhaling her scent. He didn't want to cry, but he wasn't sure he was strong enough not to.

When he reached the Long's house, Gilbert wasn't in a good mood, so finding a truck blocking the driveway didn't make him happy. He didn't recognize it, so it wasn't one of the brothers. It also wasn't Richard's truck.

Gilbert parked by the sidewalk and got out. He looked around, wondering if Marie and Richard had visitors. Usually, the only people who came around were their sons, although Gilbert knew they had more family in town. They just weren't very close to them.

Gilbert moved toward the house. Before he could reach the front door, he heard the truck door open. He was surprised, because he hadn't noticed anyone sitting in it, but then he hadn't checked.

"Excuse me?" a man called out.

Gilbert didn't want to talk to anyone, but he still stopped and turned to face the guy.

He was big and heavily muscled, looking like he spent most of his time in the gym. He wasn't Gilbert's type, although Gilbert could admit the man was handsome. His blond hair was short and spiked up with enough gel that Gilbert was pretty sure not even the strongest wind could mess it up. His jaw was square, his eyebrows carefully plucked. His muscles looked like *they* had muscles, and they stretched the t-shirt he was wearing so much that Gilbert wondered if it was about to explode.

"Yes?" he asked.

"Sorry to bother you." The man smiled, but it didn't reach his eyes. "I'm looking for Richie."

If the guy had been looking for any other brother, Gilbert wouldn't have been alarmed. Even though he knew very little about what had brought Richie back home, he knew enough.

He looked the man up and down. Was this Francis? He didn't look like Richie's type, either, but then what did Gilbert know? Just because he didn't find Francis attractive didn't mean no one did.

"I have no idea where he is," he said.

The man frowned. "Are you sure?"

"I am. Why are you looking for him? Who are you?"

Francis shook his head. "I'm just worried about him. He disappeared, and I haven't heard from him in days. I wanted to make sure he was okay."

"I wouldn't know. He never came home."

"Are you one of his brothers?"

He had to know that wasn't the case. Gilbert looked nothing like the Long brothers. Still, Gilbert had no intention of giving Francis any more information. He crossed his arms over his chest. "I already told you Richie wasn't here. I think you should leave."

"And I told you I was worried about him."

"I'm sure he'll call you."

Francis tightened his hands into fists. He looked like he wanted to hit Gilbert, which wouldn't surprise him. He just hoped Francis wouldn't because he doubted that he'd be standing by the end of it. He wanted to protect Richie, but he wasn't an idiot. He wouldn't stand a chance against Francis, and not just because he was human and less sturdy than a shifter. Francis was tall, no doubt over six feet tall, and just as wide because of his muscles. On the other hand, Gilbert barely reached five foot ten, and while he wasn't out of shape, he was nowhere near as muscled as Francis. It might not mean anything if Francis didn't know how to use his muscles, but still. He had enough power to hurt Gilbert.

Thankfully, Francis made an obvious effort to relax. He even smiled again, which was more creepy than reassuring. "I'm sure you're right," he said. "Still, if you hear from him, will you give me a call?"

Richie wanted to say no, but if it got Francis out of here faster, he'd say yes. He nodded curtly and watched as Francis reached for his jeans' back pocket. He took out a wallet, opened it, and slid out a business card. He offered it to Gilbert, who almost snorted when he saw that Francis was a personal trainer.

What else could he have been?

Gilbert put the business card into his pocket. "I'll let Richie know if he contacts us."

"You do that. Tell him I'm worried about him and that I miss him."

Gilbert was pretty sure that wasn't the case, but he stayed silent. He also didn't move, staring at Francis until he finally got the hint and went back to his truck. He climbed inside and started the engine, and Gilbert still stayed where he was. He only moved after he couldn't see Francis's truck anymore.

He turned toward the house and strode to the front door. He hoped Francis hadn't tried knocking, because he could imagine how terrifying that would have been for Richie. He quickly knocked, then opened the door. "It's me," he called out.

Richard appeared at the living room door. "Who were you

talking to? I was about to come out and see what was happening."

Gilbert grimaced. "You wouldn't have wanted to do that. Trust me. Is Richie here?"

Richard frowned. "In the kitchen with his mother. We had a bit of a talk, and they got emotional."

"And you didn't stay to comfort them?"

Richard shrugged. "I could tell they needed time on their own. Besides, I was emotional, too."

The fact that Richie had talked to his parents was good, but Gilbert was afraid that what had just happened with Francis would ruin everything. Still, it wasn't his place to keep this information from Richie.

He walked to the kitchen, Richard right behind him. Richie and his mother were sitting at the counter, softly talking, but they both looked up when they heard him. Marie smiled and got to her feet while Richie stayed where he was.

Marie hugged Gilbert. "I'll get the casserole from the fridge. Or can you stay for a bit?"

Gilbert wasn't sure. "Actually, I need to tell Richie something." He took the business card out of his pocket. "When I got here, there was a truck parked in front of the house. The guy inside was looking for you, and he gave me his business card."

Gilbert offered Richie the card, but Richie wouldn't take it. Instead, he stared at it, his eyes wide and his skin pale. His reaction was enough to tell Gilbert that Richie hadn't wanted Francis to come, whatever Francis might think or want everyone to believe.

When Richie made no move to take the card, Richard plucked it from Gilbert's fingers. He looked at it, and his expression shifted to anger. "That bastard was here?"

Gilbert nodded. "He was sitting in the truck, blocking the drive. He got out when he saw me and asked me if Richie was here. I told him I hadn't seen him and that he hadn't come home," Gilbert added in a rush when Richie started to scramble off his stool. "I told him no one had heard from you. I don't know if he believed me, but he left."

Richie sucked in a breath, then another. "I have to go."

Thankfully, his father was there. He grabbed Richie's arm, and Richie stiffened. His father released him right away, but it had been enough to stop Richie from running out. "We knew he was going to come here to look for you," he said. "You expected it, so this is nothing you have to worry about."

"He's going to hurt one of you."

"He's not. The only person he wants to hurt is you, but he won't find you. Your mother and I, along with your brothers, will make sure of that. We'll keep you safe."

"I'll do everything I can to keep you safe, too," Gilbert said. He wasn't sure what had made him say it, but he was serious. The Longs, including Richie, were his family.

"You don't understand. He's—he could easily hurt any of you, and I'll never forgive myself if that happens. I can't stay here."

Richie's mother took both his hands. Richie didn't react to her the way he had to his father but instead allowed her to hold him. "Please. Stay. I promise we'll keep you safe and that we'll be safe, too," she said.

Richie still looked like he wanted nothing more than to run away, so Gilbert was surprised when he nodded. "I'll stay," Richie murmured.

Gilbert couldn't help but wonder if it was a lie.

CHAPTER THREE

R ichie needed to leave the house. So far, he'd made do with the clothes his brothers had lent him. He'd used his parents' toiletries. Everything he'd needed, they'd given him, but it was getting old fast. Richie wanted to buy new clothes and wear things he liked. He wanted to choose his shampoo, something he hadn't been allowed to do in years. He'd left Francis to get his life back, but had he?

Since he'd arrived more than a week ago, he'd stayed inside the house. He'd made himself a prisoner, and he wanted that to end. The problem was that he was terrified.

He hadn't been allowed to do anything on his own in years. Francis did all the shopping for them, and that included Richie's clothes. Richie wasn't even sure he knew how to shop anymore, but his parents were worried, and frankly, so was he. He'd wanted to start a new life, to be free, yet, here he was.

So today, he was leaving the house.

"I could stay with you," his mother said from the driver's seat of her car.

She'd had to give him a ride because he still didn't have a car, but then, he hadn't had one in two years. It would be a while before he could buy one, but he couldn't wait. He wanted to be independent, no matter how much it scared him. Besides, he'd need a car to find a job. In such a small town, one couldn't go anywhere without one, not without a public transit system.

He wanted to accept his mother's offer, but he also didn't. "I'll be fine. It's just the mall." And it was pretty small.

His mother still looked worried. "Of course, but after everything you've been through, it would be understandable for you to feel unsafe."

And that was one more reason Richie hadn't wanted to tell his parents what had happened to him. "I'm not weak. I can defend myself."

But that was a lie, wasn't it? He hadn't been able to defend himself against Francis. He hadn't even been able to leave him. Instead, he'd stayed with him for three years, and he'd allowed him to do whatever he wanted.

"I never said you were weak. No one thinks that. But since that man came looking for you at the house, I'm a bit scared he'll find you here."

"Even if he does, he won't do anything, not in public." As he spoke, Richie remembered several times when Francis had hurt him in public. They hadn't been the worst occasions, but Richie had gone home with bruises, usually on his arms, and once they were home, things had gotten worse.

But they wouldn't today. Today, he was going home to his parents, and they'd be happy to see him. They'd make sure he was okay, his mother would prepare dinner, and he'd be able to relax. That was what he had to keep in mind. He was anxious, but he could do this, and he wouldn't run back home until he had. He was an adult man, and he had to act like it.

His mother stopped the car in front of the mall. Richie looked up and tried to swallow, but his mouth was dry.

"No one would think badly if you decided to stay home," his mother murmured.

Richie desperately wanted to accept her offer, but instead, he shook his head. "You can pick me up in a few hours. I promise I'll be fine."

His mother didn't look convinced, but thankfully, she didn't try to stop him. He took a deep breath, then, before he could change his mind, opened the passenger door. He slipped out, closed it, and walked toward the mall without looking back. Richie couldn't, not when he was sure that if he did, he'd run back to the car and go home with his mother.

Thankfully, he'd chosen to come in the middle of the day, so there weren't a lot of people around. There were still more than he liked, but then, he'd never enjoyed crowds. He knew what he needed, so he also knew where to go. He'd been planning this outing since yesterday, and he'd made a list, both of items he wanted to buy and of shops that sold them.

Everything went well in the first shop. Richie bought a few pairs of jeans and several t-shirts, smiling as he did so. He couldn't remember the last time he'd been allowed to wear a graphic t-shirt, and he felt a little bit more like himself at the thought that he soon would.

Things started going wrong when he left the shop. He couldn't shake the feeling that someone was watching him, no matter how many times he looked around to find that person. He knew he was being paranoid and that there was no way Francis was here, but what if he was? He could have been watching the house and followed the car when Richie and his mother had left earlier. If he had, he'd seen Richie was here alone, and he might be waiting for him somewhere, hiding until the right moment.

Richie stopped, clutching the bag with his new clothes. He couldn't see Francis anywhere, but what if he was about to grab Richie and drag him to his car to take him home to his apartment? Would Richie be able to fight? Or would he go along with it because that was what he'd always done?

"Hi," someone said.

Richie jumped. His heart raced, and he glanced around to find an exit, but before he could, Gilbert appeared in front of him. Richie sucked in a breath, telling himself that he was safe. Gilbert wasn't Francis, and, more importantly, he was his mate. There was no way he'd hurt Richie.

If only Richie truly believed that.

Gilbert had been smiling, but with Richie not answering, his smile turned to a frown. "Richie? Is everything okay?"

Richie didn't want Gilbert or anyone else to be worried about him. He tried to stand up straighter and smile, but it felt like a grimace, and there was nothing he could do about it. "I'm fine."

Gilbert didn't look convinced. "You were panicking. Did I scare you? Because if I did, I'm sorry. I should have known better. I thought you'd seen me, which is why I didn't think about it."

Richie hated that it was so easy for him to get scared, especially by people who wanted to help him and cared about him. "I'm fine. Just a little spooked, but it doesn't have anything to do with you," Richie confessed.

He was tired of keeping this a secret. He didn't want Gilbert to think he was weak, but they were mates, even though Gilbert didn't know. He should be aware of everything Richie was hiding before Richie told him about being mates. Richie didn't know if he'd ever be able to and if he'd ever trust Gilbert enough to let him know, but maybe this was one way to make sure Gilbert would be good for him. If Richie told him what he'd allowed Francis to do to him for three years and Gilbert despised him, Richie would never have to tell him he was his mate. He'd know for sure what kind of person Gilbert was, and right now, he needed that certainty.

"I thought Francis had found me," he said. "I was afraid he'd hurt me."

Gilbert's eyes widened. "You think he's here?"

"Not really. It just feels like it, you know?"

"And you didn't want to get hurt."

Richie had to look away. "Not again. I allowed him to hurt me enough, and I don't want to go through that ever again."

Gilbert slowly nodded. "Well, I don't know if Francis is

here, but I can stay with you just to be sure." His focus moved to the bag Richie was holding. "Did you need to buy anything else?"

"I want something to drink before I do." Richie's mouth felt like the desert, and his legs were shaky. He had to sit for a bit before he crumbled.

"Why don't we sit down at the food court and get something to drink and maybe to eat?"

Richie nodded and allowed Gilbert to steer him toward the food court. He didn't care what they ate or drank. He just wanted to sit down. He was going to tell Gilbert everything, and that thought was petrifying. It might be even scarier than having Francis find him.

Gilbert took care of everything and even kept an eye on Richie as he ordered their food and drinks. While he was away, Richie gave himself a pep talk. He never wanted to think about what he was about to tell Gilbert again, and hopefully, he wouldn't have to talk about it once this was over. His parents knew everything he wanted them to know, as did his brothers. It would be humiliating enough to have to tell Gilbert, and he wasn't planning to tell anyone else.

He wasn't even sure he'd manage to tell Gilbert everything. But maybe he didn't have to. Maybe only telling Gilbert most of it would be enough. It would provide Gilbert with everything he needed to know about Richie, and his reaction would tell Richie what he needed to know about his mate.

Gilbert was surprised that Richie was still sitting at the table he'd chosen by the time Gilbert got their food and drinks. He'd only gotten sodas and fries, but hopefully, it would be enough to soothe Richie. Gilbert suspected Richie wanted company more than he wanted food, but it would give both of them something to do with their hands.

He placed everything on the table in front of Richie and sat in an empty chair. He wasn't quite sure what to say, so he snatched a fry and stuffed it into his mouth.

"He abused me," Richie blurted out.

Gilbert almost choked on his fry, but he managed to swallow it. He gave himself a moment to drink some of his soda, trying to think what he could say. He'd suspected Francis had abused Richie, but he hadn't thought Richie would admit it to anyone, let alone him. He and Richie didn't know each other. Sure, they'd seen each other a few times, and Richie's family trusted Gilbert, but Gilbert was surprised to find that was enough for Richie to open up to him.

He didn't want to break that trust, and he wanted to react in the best way possible, although he wasn't sure what that way was.

"I'm sorry that happened to you," he ended up saying.

Richie took a fry, but he didn't eat it. He stared at it instead, and Gilbert wondered if he was going to say anything else or if this was it.

"He wasn't like that in the beginning," Richie eventually said. "When I first met him, he was sweet and gentle. Now, I know it was a show to get me to fall in love with him."

Gilbert didn't know much about abuse, but he suspected a lot of abusers behaved that way. They needed to reel in their victims and get their claws into them before they could start abusing them.

"Everything was mostly fine for the first year," Richie continued. "He did weird things, but it was easy to ignore them. Then, he started getting violent." Richie swallowed heavily. "In the beginning, he kept accusing me of looking at other guys, but it quickly escalated to him thinking I was cheating on him and disrespecting him. From there, he started hitting me every time I did something he didn't like." Richie softly snorted. "By the end, it was enough for me to wear clothes he didn't approve of for him to hit me."

"But you got out," Gilbert said gently.

"I still don't know how I found the strength to do it. I told him I wanted to cut my hair." Richie reached up and tugged on the strand of hair that fell in front of his face. "I never liked it long, but he did. I told him I wanted to cut it, and he freaked out."

And he'd beaten Richie over a haircut. Gilbert had to take a deep breath, because he felt like he was about to explode. He wanted to find Francis and make him feel the way he'd made Richie feel, but Richie needed him. Besides, Gilbert wouldn't know where to start looking for Francis.

"He apologized afterward. He told me it was my fault because I knew better than to cut my hair. I knew better than to provoke him into hitting me, and I did. I knew what would happen, but I did it anyway. I should have behaved better."

Dammit. Gilbert wasn't surprised Richie felt that way, but he wished Richie understood none of this was his fault. He wasn't sure it was his place to say anything about it or if Richie would believe him. Probably not if Francis had been telling him it was his fault for the past three years.

"I should have left when he hit me the first time, but I was weak."

That was the one thing Gilbert wouldn't allow Richie to say about himself. "You're not weak."

"What do you call it, then? I stayed with him even though he hurt me. I knew he wasn't going to change, yet it took me three years to get away."

"It doesn't mean you're weak. He isolated you from your family, didn't he? You said you moved away, and I never met you."

"He didn't want me to spend time with my family."

"Because he was afraid he'd lose you, and he was right. He did in the end. It doesn't matter how long you were with him.

You were never weak. You were abused and hurt and scared, and that has nothing to do with strength."

"How can you say it doesn't? I wouldn't have allowed him to hurt me if I hadn't been weak."

"Did you love him?"

"I did. Sometimes, I still do. I love the man he was initially, and I guess I hoped I'd see that man again. When I realized he'd never existed . . ." Richie shrugged. "I left. But I still should have left way sooner than I did."

"You left when you were ready to. I know that nothing I can say will change your mind, but I don't think you're weak. I think you were taken advantage of and that it should never have happened to you. But it doesn't reflect on you. All of this tells me the kind of man Francis is, not what kind of man *you* are."

Gilbert might not know a lot about abusive situations and how the people who were abused felt, but he was convinced of what he'd said. He'd never think of anyone in this situation as weak. The fact that Richie felt that way meant that Francis still had his hooks into him, and Gilbert wanted to help him get rid of them. It would take time, but he suspected it wouldn't happen as long as Francis was still around.

"Has he come around the house again?" he asked.

"No. I haven't seen him." Richie hesitated. "But he's been calling and texting," he added in a whisper.

Gilbert wasn't surprised. "You should get a new phone, then."

"How? I don't have any money. I'm dependent on my parents like I was when I was a kid. I had to ask them for money because I don't have anything left. Francis didn't allow me to work for the past two years, and he had control over the accounts. I don't have a car because he sold it, saying I wouldn't need it anyway since I wasn't working."

Gilbert took a chance and reached for Richie's hand on the

table. Richie didn't pull his away, but he stared at Gilbert's as if he wasn't quite sure what was happening. Maybe he wasn't. Gilbert wasn't sure himself, but he wanted to do something for Richie.

He wouldn't be able to make Francis disappear from Richie's life, but maybe he could help Richie in his next steps to a new life. "I'll get you a phone."

Richie's eyes widened, and he pulled his hand away. "I can't allow you to do that. You don't owe me anything."

"It doesn't have anything to do with owing. I want to get you a phone. I can afford to, so you don't have to worry about that."

"I can't take your money."

"Then don't take the money. Take the phone. You can give me the money back when you start working, or never. I really don't care."

"Why?"

"Because you're my best friend's brother. Because your family welcomed me when I needed them, and they've been there for me more than my own family has. Because they're my family now, too, which means you are."

"It doesn't make sense," Richie murmured.

"Does it have to? I understand you don't trust me and that you don't know me. I'm okay with that. But we're going to be in each other's lives, and I want you to get to know me. If you want, you can ask your brothers about me. They'll tell you everything you want to know. For now, though, I'd like to help you the way I would my sibling if I had one."

Gilbert was an only child, and he'd never have siblings, or at least, that was what he'd always thought. When he'd met Laurie, though, he'd found a brother and, along with him, more brothers and parents. Richie had been away, but he was back, and Gilbert had every intention of being part of his life. He didn't understand why it was so important to him, but that wouldn't stop him. The only thing that could was Richie himself, and Gilbert hoped he wouldn't.

None of this made sense. Richie didn't understand why Gilbert was doing it. He was Laurie's best friend, not Richie's. They didn't even know each other. Why would Gilbert want to help him like that?

But Richie had to remember that Gilbert wasn't just his baby brother's best friend. He was also his mate, even though he didn't know about it. He was human, so he couldn't sense it, but that didn't mean he didn't feel drawn to Richie. Maybe that was why he wanted to help. Deep inside, he knew what they were to each other, and he wanted to take care of Richie.

Richie's first instinct was to say no, get to his feet, and leave. He wanted to take care of himself. But Gilbert wasn't Francis, and he wasn't Richie's parents. He was Richie's *mate*, and once that would have meant everything to Richie.

Gilbert was nothing like Francis. Richie might not know Gilbert well, but what he did know about him was enough to convince him of that. It didn't mean he trusted Gilbert, but he certainly trusted him more than he did Francis.

Richie wasn't ready for a relationship. He didn't know if he ever would be, which was one of the reasons he hadn't told Gilbert he was his mate. It wouldn't be fair to tell him only to explain he didn't want to be with him. Besides, he hoped that would eventually change. It wasn't fair to ask Gilbert to wait for him when it might take years, which was why Richie was planning on keeping it to himself. For now, though, that wasn't what he was focused on.

He wanted to trust Gilbert, but he didn't know if he could. He didn't want to offend Gilbert, and he hoped his mate would understand. Richie suspected he would. He didn't think Richie was weak for staying with Francis, and Richie believed him.

The problem was that Richie did. He hadn't seen who Francis really was until it was too late, and when he had, he'd stayed with the man. What if Gilbert was just as great at hiding? What if Richie let him in and Gilbert turned around and hurt him?

Logically, Richie knew that wouldn't be the case. It was his fear speaking, but he couldn't push past it. There had to be something defective in him that he hadn't seen how Francis was. He couldn't trust himself a second time, which was why he couldn't give Gilbert a chance.

"I promise I don't expect anything from you, not even for you to repay me," Gilbert said. "But I want to give you the opportunity to get away from Francis."

"I *am* away from Francis." Richie ate a fry, even though it was cold.

Francis hadn't allowed him to have fries or any kind of fast food when they'd been together. He hadn't wanted Richie to get fat. Eating fries and drinking soda felt like a *fuck you* to Francis, and it made Richie almost feel giddy. It also scared him, and he kept looking around, expecting Francis to pop out to yell at him for eating them.

"Physically, yes. But he can still reach you. If he's calling you and you have to see those calls and texts, you're not free of him. You don't have to do this if you don't want to, but I think it would be good for you."

"But I wouldn't know what he's planning."

"Wouldn't you? Because you knew he was going to try to come to your parents' house. You know he's probably going to try again."

Gilbert was right. There was no way Francis was giving up this easily. That meant he'd come to the house again and that he'd attempt to talk to Richie. Richie couldn't allow that to happen.

Over the past three years, he'd tried leaving Francis a few times. In the beginning, he'd been open about it. After the first time Francis had hit him, he'd packed his bags, ready to go home. Francis had begged him to stay. He'd apologized and promised he'd never do something like that again.

But he had. Richie had decided to stay and give Francis a second chance, and Francis had broken his trust again. He'd hit Richie, and he'd pleaded to have another chance. Time and time again, Richie had given in until he was afraid that if he didn't, Francis would kill him.

Once Richie had been too tired and scared to care about those threats, Francis had moved on. If he couldn't scare Richie into staying by threatening to kill him, he threatened to kill his family. It had worked, and Richie had stayed.

Until he hadn't. He still wasn't sure what was different about this time. He'd wanted a haircut, and Francis had freaked out. He'd beaten Richie, had made him bleed and had blamed him for it. He'd said that Richie had known better than to mention a haircut. He'd pulled on Richie's hair, something he wouldn't have been able to do if Richie had cut it.

And Richie had realized just how much control Francis had over him. Richie had been so afraid to provoke Francis into hitting him that he'd done his best to avoid it. That meant not arguing when Francis did something Richie didn't like. It meant going along with everything Francis wanted, including wearing the clothes he said Richie should wear, eating the food that would keep Richie thin the way Francis liked. Richie's life wasn't his own anymore, and he'd wanted to die.

That was what had made him realize he needed to get out. No matter how scary it was, if he stayed, he wouldn't have much time left. He wanted to see his family again, and that had given him the push he needed.

And now, here he was. He didn't have anything to his name, but he was free. He could find a job he liked, move into his own apartment, even cut his hair without Francis having anything to do with those decisions. Having so much freedom after the past few years felt overwhelming in the best of ways.

And Richie wasn't alone. He had people who wanted to help him any way they could, including Gilbert. Richie might still be wary of him, but what would change if he accepted Gilbert's offer to buy him a phone? If Gilbert tried to use it against him, Richie would give the phone back. If that wasn't enough, Richie just had to mention something to his family, and Gilbert would be out of his life.

He looked at Gilbert, who was staring at him silently. "All right."

Gilbert smiled. "You'll let me buy you a phone?"

"I will. You're right that by keeping this one, I'm allowing Francis to keep control over me." It wasn't just because of the phone calls and texts, either. Francis had bought Richie this phone, and like always, Richie hadn't had a say in it. He wanted to be able to choose his own clothes, but also his phone.

Gilbert beamed. "That's great. Shall we go?"

Richie felt giddy again as they left the food court. He was still terrified, but he was doing his best to ignore it, and he almost managed. It was easy to focus on all the new things he was buying instead of obsessing over what Gilbert would do next, so Richie did just that.

He chose his phone, got a new number, and allowed Gilbert to pay for it. He didn't protest again, not even when he cringed at the cost. Gilbert wouldn't have offered if he couldn't afford it, right?

As soon as they were out of the shop, Richie took his old phone out and turned it off. He resisted the urge to read the texts Francis had sent. He never would, and it felt like a weight had lifted from his shoulders.

"You said something about a haircut," Gilbert said.

Richie didn't want to think about the past, but he wasn't surprised Gilbert had questions. "I did. Wanting one is why Francis did this," he said, gesturing to his face. He was almost healed, but there were still traces of the bruises.

Gilbert pointed at something. "Want to get a haircut, then?"

Richie swallowed. His first instinct was to say no. Then he reached up and touched the fringe that fell in front of his eyes. He'd never liked that. When his hair became long enough to fall in front of his face, he usually had it cut, but he hadn't been allowed to in several months.

Now, he was. He was allowed to do anything he wanted because there was no one controlling him anymore. The only one who had control over Richie was Richie himself.

Gilbert didn't think Richie would accept. Now that he knew how significant a haircut was to him, he wouldn't be surprised if Richie didn't feel comfortable having one, at least right now. But he'd seen how uncomfortable Richie's hair made him, and he'd wanted Richie to know he could cut it. He didn't need anyone's permission, but Gilbert was ready to pay for it since he was short on money.

Richie tugged on his hair. "You think I should cut it?"

"What I think doesn't matter. The only one who should have a say in that decision is you. I just wanted you to know that if you do want to cut it, I'm more than happy to pay for it."

Richie grimaced. "I don't like feeling like I owe you things."

Probably because it gave Gilbert some kind of power over him. Gilbert understood, but he wasn't sure there was anything he could do about it. Beyond telling Richie he really didn't mind, what else could he say? It was a question of trust—of whether or not Richie would be able to trust that Gilbert wouldn't hurt him the way Francis had. Gilbert wasn't offended that Richie thought he might.

They didn't know each other, and it made sense that Richie was wary of anyone he didn't know well, especially after the way things had started between him and Francis. For all Richie knew, Gilbert might be playing nice because he was like Francis and wanted to pull him closer.

"If you feel more comfortable with it, I'm sure your parents wouldn't hesitate to pay me back, even today if it makes you feel better."

"I don't want to owe them anything, either."

"I understand that, but if you're more comfortable having them pay for things, it's fine."

Richie looked at the hairdresser Gilbert had noticed. It was clear he wanted to get his haircut, but several things were apparently working against that. Gilbert stayed silent, giving Richie the time and space he needed to make his decision. After what Francis had done, Gilbert didn't want to influence Richie in any way.

"Are you sure about this?" Richie asked.

"I am. I already told you I owe your family a lot."

"But I still don't know why."

Gilbert didn't want to tell anyone about it because he didn't want to have to think about it, but this was Richie. Even though they didn't know each other, Gilbert trusted him. It didn't make sense, but then emotions and feelings often didn't. "I lost my mother when I was thirteen. She died of cancer."

"I'm sorry." Richie's expression was soft, and he truly looked like he was sorry for what had happened.

It made Gilbert smile. "Thank you. Things weren't easy after that. My father didn't know how to deal with me, or how to take care of the house, things like that. I had to step into my mother's role. I took care of myself in the years after that. When I was eighteen, I came out to my father. I was afraid to do it sooner because I didn't know how he'd react."

"How did he react?" Richie asked when Gilbert didn't continue.

Gilbert licked his dry lips. "Not well. He didn't accept it. He thought I was gay because he had to raise me on his own for years. I told him that was ridiculous, but he was convinced, and he still is. He doesn't accept it. It's not the only problem between us, but it's the main one, and the reason I didn't talk to him for months. I can count on the fingers of one hand how many times I talked to him in the past two years."

"I'm sorry."

Gilbert shrugged. "I've gotten used to it. I don't expect my father ever to accept me, and it's okay. But your brother was there for me when that happened, and he took me home. Your parents and your brothers adopted me. I don't know where I'd be if it weren't for them. They treated me like a son and a brother, which means you're kind of my brother, too."

For some reason, that made Richie grimace. "I suppose," he said.

"But even if you weren't related to them, they care about you. They want you to be happy, and I do, too. Even though there's nothing I can do to make it happen, I can help you where I can, and in this situation, I can."

Richie looked at the hairdresser again. "I think I'll do it," he murmured.

Gilbert had to force himself not to grin. "Good. Let's head that way, all right? You can change your mind at any time."

Richie snorted. "I'm pretty sure that once they start cutting my hair, there's not much I'll be able to do to stop it."

"Probably not, but if you freak out, I'll be outside."

Richie glanced at Gilbert as they walked. "You don't have to wait. You could go."

"I'm not going anywhere unless you want me to."

He half expected Richie to tell him to leave, but he didn't. Instead, he nodded. "I'd like for you to stay," he said.

"Then I will." He pointed at a bench outside the hairdresser. "I'll be right there when you're done."

"Thank you."

Gilbert wanted to brush off Richie's thanks, but he didn't. This was important to Richie, and he wanted Richie to be happy and feel at ease with him. "You're welcome. I'm sure you'll be able to pay me back the favor when I need something."

Richie barked out a laugh. "So you do have a reason for doing this."

"Maybe." Gilbert winked, even though he wasn't a wink kind of guy. He just wanted Richie to understand he was joking.

Richie disappeared inside the shop, and Gilbert settled on the bench to wait for him after paying for the cut. He'd wait the rest of the day if he had to, but he didn't think he would. It might have taken Richie a while to make this decision, but now that he had, Gilbert thought he'd go through with it. And if he didn't, well, Gilbert would be there for him. They might have to deal with an awful haircut, but that wouldn't be a problem.

Gilbert didn't have to wait long for Richie to come back. When he did, there was a shy smile on his face, and he looked bashful. He reached out to pull on his hair, but it was gone. The shorter hair made his features appear sharper than before, but Gilbert thought it made him look even more handsome. Not that Richie had cared about that when he'd decided he wanted to cut his hair, but still. It was good to see him feel better about himself, even though he was clearly still uncomfortable.

"Feel better?" Gilbert asked.

"I do. It's weird, but I'll get used to it again." He looked at Gilbert. "I don't think I'd have had the courage if you hadn't pushed me."

"I didn't push you. I just gave you the opportunity to do what you wanted to, and you did it. You did all of this yourself, and you should be proud."

"I think I might be."

"Good." Richie needed to be proud of himself, but Gilbert understood why he might not feel that way. He would, in time. Gilbert would make sure of it.

"I don't know how to thank you."

"Don't. Seeing you happy is enough for me. I wasn't sure how to help you, knowing that your entire family is there for you, so I'm glad I could do at least this."

Richie slowly nodded. "It means a lot more than you'll ever realize."

Gilbert wasn't sure that was the case, or maybe it was. It didn't matter. Gilbert would do everything he could to keep Richie happy, even though he didn't understand why he felt that way. He didn't think the reason mattered, anyway. Wanting to keep Richie happy wasn't a bad thing, so it was easy for Gilbert to give in and do just that.

CHAPTER FOUR

R ichie was feeling better, and he could hardly believe it. He was still afraid Francis would pop out to drag him home, or rather, to his apartment. He still looked around when he left the house, just in case Francis was there. But not having to feel his phone vibrate every time Francis sent him a text or tried to call had lifted a weight from Richie's shoulders. He'd never be able to thank Gilbert enough for that.

He'd never be able to thank Gilbert for many things, including his new haircut. Every time he walked past a mirror, Richie found himself stopping. His hair hadn't been this short for almost three years, and it felt weird. He found himself reaching to tug on it several times a day, and he was having a hard time dropping that habit. But he supposed he would, in time.

For now, he reached up to pull on his hair. He was stretched out on his bed, wondering what to do with his day, but he didn't have an answer. He had nothing to do because he didn't have a job. That would take time, too.

He would do many things eventually, but for now, there was one thing he wanted to focus on. It was time for him to move forward, and while there was nothing he could do to get himself an apartment or a car, he could find a job, and more importantly, he could welcome Gilbert into his life.

Although Gilbert was already part of Richie's life. He visited Richie's parents often, and just like Gilbert had said, they treated him like a son. It wasn't like they didn't have enough sons already, which meant they truly liked Gilbert. In Richie's eyes, that meant Gilbert was a good person. His parents and his brothers wouldn't like him otherwise.

He was still afraid he was wrong. He didn't know Gilbert, although he realized it was partly his fault. He hadn't spent a lot of time with Gilbert because he'd been terrified. What was he supposed to do with the knowledge that Gilbert was his mate? Gilbert had a right to know, since it involved him, too, but Richie couldn't tell him before he was sure Gilbert wouldn't hurt him.

But even though Richie had kept his distance, Gilbert had slowly worked himself into Richie's life. They hadn't spent time alone since the mall, but Gilbert always had a smile for Richie. It had gotten to the point that Laurie had noticed something, but thankfully, he hadn't asked yet.

Richie might have a hard time trusting Gilbert, but his family didn't. Richie trusted them more than he trusted himself right now, which meant he'd decided that Gilbert was a good person and that he should be in Richie's life.

Every time they spoke, Richie realized how well they fit together. It wasn't unexpected, but it was still strange to feel that way. When he'd left Francis, he hadn't believed he'd feel like this for a long time, if ever. He certainly hadn't expected to consider being in a relationship with someone so soon after running away.

But Gilbert was nothing like Francis. Richie wanted more from his life than what he had right now, and the only thing stopping him from getting it was his fears. It wasn't easy to work through them, and he suspected they'd be there for a long time, but maybe he could ignore them.

The problem was that he wasn't at his best. Would Gilbert even consider dating him? Richie couldn't make any promises, and he felt it was unfair. He wasn't even sure he was the kind of guy Gilbert usually dated. Maybe he should find out more about Gilbert before making any decisions.

He sat up. There was only one person who could tell him what he wanted to know about Gilbert, and he happened to be in the house right now. Surely Richie should spend more time with his niece?

Richie hopped off the bed. He straightened his t-shirt but didn't bother putting on socks as he left his bedroom. He couldn't help but notice that he hadn't hesitated. He was starting to feel more at home with every day he spent in the house, and it felt good.

He rushed downstairs, knowing where he'd find Laurie and Melissa. When they visited, they spent time in the kitchen with Richie and Laurie's mom. It was great to watch her interacting with Melissa. After raising seven boys, she was over-the-moon happy to have a little girl in her life.

Richie heard voices before he reached the kitchen, and it made him smile. His mother was cooing at Melissa, so he wasn't surprised to find Melissa in her highchair, sucking on her fist. Laurie was sitting at the table, drinking a cup of coffee and looking amused.

He glanced up when he heard Richie and smiled at him. His smile was more natural than it would have been right after Richie had arrived. He and the other brothers were getting used to having Richie back in their lives. Laurie was one of the brothers who visited the house more often because of Melissa, so he and Richie were getting close.

"Hi there," Laurie said. "I was wondering what you were up to."

"Nothing much. I need to find a job." Richie plopped into the chair next to Laurie's.

"Is that a good idea?" Richie's mother asked without looking at him.

She and Richie's father had been babying him, and while he didn't resent them for that and even understood why they were doing it, he also wished they'd stop. "I can't exactly live here for the rest of my life without helping around at the very least."

She looked at him, a frown on her face. "No one said anything about that. Besides, you *are* helping."

"With the chores, sure." Richie had taken to cooking several times a week, although only when he and his parents were alone. It was too much to cook for all his brothers, especially with how much food some of them ate. "I want to do more, though. It's not fair that you and Dad have to pay for everything for me, including food and new clothes."

His mother turned around to face him. "We're more than happy to pay for you."

Richie sighed. This wasn't why he'd come downstairs, but he wouldn't be able to avoid this conversation for long. Besides, he didn't want to. The thought of finding a job that would expose him terrified him, but it was something he had to do. "I know you don't mind. I'm thankful you welcomed me back home and aren't demanding anything from me, and I always will be. But I can't keep on hiding. I'm an adult, almost thirty. I can't spend the rest of my life allowing you to pay for me."

"I'm just worried," his mother murmured.

"I am, too. But I let Francis take too much from me. I can't continue this way. As it is, his presence is still too strong in my life, and I don't like it."

Richie's mother nodded and turned back to Melissa. Richie knew the conversation wasn't over, but he was relieved they wouldn't continue it now. He wanted to have a plan in place before he talked to his parents about his next steps.

For now, he turned to Laurie, who was staring at him.

"I'm impressed," Laurie said.

Richie blinked. "Why?"

"I don't know that I would be as brave as you in your situation. I think I'd keep on hiding in this house until I'm sure the guy I dated was behind bars."

Richie snorted. "I doubt Francis will ever be behind bars. He's too sneaky."

"Then what? You're going to go out there and risk him finding you?"

Richie wanted to say no, but that wasn't how he'd get his life back. "Maybe. I don't want to talk about him right now, though."

"Of course. I'm sorry I brought it up. I'm just in awe of you."

Richie didn't understand that, so he was more than happy to move the topic to something else — or in this case, someone else. "I wanted to ask you about Gilbert."

Laurie looked surprised for a moment before the corners of his lips curled into a smile. "I knew you were interested in him."

Richie didn't like being so obvious, but this was Laurie. He was Richie's brother, and he wouldn't use the knowledge that Richie liked Gilbert against him. "I'm not sure how I feel about him, to be honest. I didn't think I'd want to be in a relationship with anyone so soon after Francis, and I don't know if I'm ready. But I like him, and he was there for me when I needed someone."

"I'm not going to push for answers. What do you want to know?"

Richie sucked in a breath. "What kind of guys does Gilbert usually date?" It was a good place to start, or at least Richie hoped so.

Gilbert smiled when he saw Laurie's car parked in front of his parents' house. It meant he and Melissa were there, and it had been too long since Gilbert had seen the kid. He and Laurie didn't have as much time to spend together now that Laurie had a mate and a child, and Gilbert missed both him and Melissa. He even missed Alexis, in spite of not knowing her that well.

He climbed out of his car and made a beeline for the front door. He gave a quick knock before pushing the door open, knowing no one expected him to knock. He still did it every time because it was what his mother would have done.

"Where is everyone?" he called out.

"Gilbert?" Marie answered.

"Who else?" Gilbert went toward the kitchen.

That was usually where he could find Marie and any visitor she had. Her sons could also be found there, stuffing their faces with her food.

Sure enough, when Gilbert reached the kitchen, Laurie and Melissa were there. She was eating something orange, and she opened her mouth when she saw him. The problem was that her mouth was full, and orange goo dribbled from her lips.

Gilbert wrinkled his nose. He was thankful he wouldn't be the one to deal with that.

"Come on, baby," Laurie said, grabbing a napkin. "You have to keep your mouth shut when you eat."

Melissa didn't care. She blew him a raspberry, spitting the orange goo all over his face. Laurie wasn't fast enough jerking back, and instead of cleaning her, he used the napkin to clean his own face.

"I don't think I'm ready for her to start eating solids," he muttered when Gilbert sat next to him.

"Is that why you're not doing this in your apartment?"

Laurie grinned. "How do you know me so well? I mean, this kitchen has seen seven toddlers. I don't think it's a problem for it to see an eighth."

"That, and you want *me* to clean up after your daughter," Laurie's mother said.

"Me? Never. But if you want to change her diaper when

she's done, feel free."

Gilbert felt himself relaxing. He always did when he was here, and he loved it. It felt more like home than the house he'd grown up in with his father.

He looked around. "Where's Richie?" Usually, Richie tended to stay in his bedroom, but not always. He was starting to come out more as time passed, which meant that when Gilbert visited, they talked. He was kind of sorry Richie was nowhere to be seen today.

For some reason, his words made Laurie smile. "Why are you asking?"

"Because I want to know where he is?" Gilbert didn't think it was such a hard question to answer.

"All right, but why do you want to know where he is?"

"Because I want to make sure he's okay. What's going on with you?"

Laurie shook his head. "Nothing. He's upstairs, but he'll come downstairs soon. We weren't sure you'd come by."

"Is my presence a problem?" It had never been, but things could change. Besides, considering Richie's situation, Gilbert wouldn't be surprised if they did. He didn't want to do anything that made Richie uncomfortable, so he was ready to leave if he had to.

"It's not. Stay right where you are," Laurie ordered.

"You shouldn't stick your nose into this," Laurie's mother said from the chair where she was feeding Melissa.

Gilbert had no idea what they were talking about, and he was afraid to ask. Sometimes this family was strange. Laurie was all but bouncing in his chair, and Gilbert didn't understand why. He leaned closer. "What's going on?"

"Richie asked about you."

Gilbert had no idea what that meant. "What do you mean?"

"He asked what kind of guys you date."

It took a moment for Gilbert's brain to comprehend the words. "Why would he ask that?"

Laurie looked at him like he was an idiot. "Why do you think? He's interested in you."

"That's not possible." The breakup with Francis was still too fresh for Richie to be interested in anyone, right? Of course, Gilbert couldn't speak for him, but he couldn't imagine Richie would want to put himself out there again after what Francis had done to him. He was dealing with the consequences of that, and while Gilbert was more than happy to be by his side and help him in any way he could, he didn't want to get his hopes up.

Because he liked Richie. It hadn't taken him long to realize he didn't like Richie like he liked the other six brothers, and he wouldn't say no to dating Richie. Keeping Richie safe and happy was more important to Gilbert than anything else, though.

"Why not? I know the two of you have been spending time together," Laurie said.

"We have, but mostly, it's been here."

"What about the mall?" Laurie's mother asked.

"Didn't you just tell Laurie to stay out of it?" Gilbert teased.

Marie glared at him. "It's my baby the two of you are talking about. I want to know what's going on in his life."

"I honestly have no idea what's happening," Gilbert told her.

"I can't believe my best friend and my brother are dating," Laurie said.

Gilbert narrowed his eyes. "We're not dating. I'm not even sure we're friends. Yes, we spend time together, and I've been helping Richie where I can, but you know Richie's situation. How can you expect him to start dating anyone?"

Laurie's smile fell, and Gilbert felt a bit guilty. Still, Laurie had to be realistic about this.

"You're not just anyone," Laurie said. "You're my best friend, and you'll treat him right. I trust you with him, and I think he trusts you with himself, too. I know about the haircut."

Gilbert was surprised Richie had told anyone what happened at the mall. "He needed one, and I paid for it. That's all there is to it."

Laurie rolled his eyes. "That's bullshit. Look, if you don't like my brother that way, it's fine. Just be honest with him."

But Gilbert did like Richie that way. That was the problem. After everything Richie had gone through, Gilbert didn't think he had a chance. He couldn't see how Richie would want to be with him, especially since they barely knew each other. They might be able to get over that by spending more time together, but he doubted Richie would want that. He barely left the house as it was, and that was perfectly okay. He needed time to rest and, more importantly, heal. Physically, he was fine now. Mentally and emotionally, it would take time.

Gilbert heard a door close upstairs. Both he and Laurie looked at the kitchen door, and Laurie's eyes went wide. "Don't tell him we were talking about this," he said.

"I have no intention of doing that. Besides, he wouldn't be happy to know you're talking behind his back."

"What was I supposed to do? You're my best friend. I can't *not* tell you about this."

Gilbert wanted to say that was bullshit, too, but Richie was already walking through the door, so he kept his mouth shut and instead looked at him.

Gilbert frowned. There was something odd about Richie, and it took Gilbert a moment to understand what it was.

Since the day at the mall, Richie's aspect had changed. It was the haircut, of course, but it was also the clothes. When Richie had arrived that first day, he'd been wearing a dress shirt and a sweater. He'd looked very proper and very different from the way he dressed now. At the mall, he'd bought jeans and graphic t-shirts, and when he wore them, he was more comfortable.

He was wearing a shirt again today, though. It was buttoned to his throat, and, paired with dress pants and nice shoes, it made him look like he had a job interview. Gilbert wondered if that was the case, but when Richie saw him, his cheeks flushed, and he sat in a chair on the other side of the table.

"Hello," he said.

Richie had styled his hair, slicking it to one side. He kept reaching for it, but the gel he'd used made it impossible to run his fingers through it. He seemed to remember it every so often and lowered his hand, only to reach up again seconds later.

Something was wrong. Gilbert wasn't sure what had happened, but he didn't like what he was seeing. He wanted Richie to be happy and comfortable, and right now, he wasn't.

Richie desperately wanted Gilbert to like him, and he hoped the clothes he was wearing would help.

Laurie had told him that Gilbert usually went out with guys who dressed up smartly. His words had been that Gilbert went out with cute librarians, so Richie had chosen clothes he thought a librarian might wear. He didn't have a lot of them, since when he'd bought his new clothes, he'd stuck with things he enjoyed wearing, but he hoped Gilbert liked what he saw anyway.

Richie was as far from a librarian as he could be. He disliked dress shirts, and he hated ties. He hadn't worn one because he'd thought it would be obvious that he didn't like it, and now, he wasn't sure this was enough.

He bit his lower lip. Since Laurie had mentioned librarians, Richie suspected Gilbert liked books. It had been a while since Richie had finished one.

He leaned back in his chair, trying to look comfortable. "Finished any good books recently?" he asked.

Laurie made a strange sound, but Richie kept his focus on Gilbert, who was gaping. Richie didn't know what that meant, and it made him uncomfortable. His skin itched, and he wanted nothing more than to go back upstairs to his room.

Instead, he forced himself to stay where he was. If he wanted Gilbert in his life, he was going to have to work for it.

"Why are you asking?" Gilbert asked.

"Why not? I'm trying to make conversation."

"I see." Gilbert wrinkled his nose. "I've been reading a book on the Chernobyl disaster."

Richie was pretty sure he knew what Gilbert was talking about. "The bomb?"

Gilbert hesitated. "The nuclear plant. But I realize the topic is boring to most people."

Richie wanted to kick himself. How had he ended up with a mate who was so much smarter than he was? "Right. Sorry."

Richie was starting to change his mind. He still wanted to spend time with Gilbert and be with him, but he was humiliating himself and doing it in front of his brother and his mother. It would be bad enough if Gilbert was the only one there. He wasn't, and Richie was starting to panic.

He swallowed. "Any other book?" he asked.

To his surprise, Gilbert shot to his feet. He briefly wondered if he'd offended Gilbert or if maybe Gilbert had decided this was horrible and he needed to go, but Gilbert was reaching for him. He paused before actually touching Richie's hand. "I'd like to talk to you," he said.

Richie wasn't sure he wanted to talk to Gilbert. How could he know what Gilbert wanted from him? Still, he could feel his brother and his mother's focus on him, and he wanted out of this kitchen. The easiest way to make that happen would be to go with Gilbert. "We can go."

Gilbert nodded and moved toward the back door. Richie followed, uncomfortable and confused. He'd been doing his best to appeal to Gilbert, but obviously, he'd failed.

Gilbert waited until Richie was outside, then closed the door. They were still in sight of the kitchen, so Richie would have help if he needed it. He didn't think he would, but he knew Gilbert had done it on purpose, and he was grateful.

Gilbert thought about Richie much more than Richie would have expected or deserved.

"What's going on?" Gilbert asked.

Had he realized what Richie was doing? "I'm not sure what you're asking." There was no way Richie could confess asking Laurie about Gilbert. It would tell Gilbert how important he was to Richie, and that would give him power.

Gilbert crossed his arms over his chest and stared. "That's a lie," he said slowly.

Richie had to stop the panic from pushing him to do something stupid. It might have been three years since he'd last been in this situation, but he could do this. He had to remember that Gilbert wasn't Francis. He wasn't even close to being similar to Francis.

"I promise it's not," he tried.

"I can see that's a lie, Richie. I don't know what's going on, but I'd like to find out. I don't like what I'm seeing."

Richie frowned. Had Laurie lied to him? Had he been making fun of him when he'd said that Gilbert dated guys who looked like librarians? Richie wouldn't have thought that of his brother, but he and Laurie hadn't been close in a while. Maybe he didn't know Laurie as well as he thought he did.

"Just tell me," Gilbert said. "I won't be angry."

"You can't know that," Richie muttered.

"All right, maybe I *will* be angry. But I promise I won't raise a hand to you."

He shouldn't have to make that kind of promise. He was Richie's mate, and Richie should have more faith in him. Besides, Gilbert was smaller than him. Even if he did try to hit Richie, it wouldn't hurt as much as it had when Francis had.

Richie swallowed. "I talked to Laurie earlier," he whispered.

Gilbert frowned and nodded. "He did mention something about that."

"Did he tell you I asked about you? That I wanted to know the kind of guys you usually date?"

"He did." Gilbert paused and looked Richie up and down. "Is that why you're dressed this way? What did Laurie tell you, exactly?"

"That you date guys who liked books and who dress like librarians. That you enjoy dress shirts and things like that. I wanted to look good for you."

Richie waited, holding his breath. He had no idea how Gilbert would react, but he was ready to run. He almost did when Gilbert reached for his face, but he forced himself to stay where he was. Even if Gilbert hit him, Richie could stand it. He'd lived through worse.

But Gilbert didn't hit Richie. Instead, he touched his hair. Richie had used a lot of gel to keep it slicked the way Laurie had said Gilbert liked, so he wasn't surprised when it took Gilbert a while to untangle it. Richie's hair felt freer when he was finally done, and when he touched it, he could push his fingers through it again.

"You don't have to do these things," Gilbert said. "I don't need you to look like a librarian." He snorted. "Besides, what does that even mean? Your brother is an asshole."

Richie felt like the bottom of his stomach dropped. "Did he lie?"

"Not exactly. He's right that I like books and that the guys I usually date look preppy. It doesn't mean I expect them to like books, and I don't just date guys who wear dress shirts."

"I wanted you to like me." Richie smoothed the shirt down on his stomach. He'd made a mess again, hadn't he?

"But don't you see? I already like you. I don't need you to wear these clothes or talk about books for me to. I like you the way you are, and you don't need to change for me. I don't *want* you to change for me."

"I should be better."

Gilbert frowned. "What does that mean? You're exactly the way you should be."

Richie shook his head. Gilbert didn't understand because he didn't know. "That's not true. I should be perfect for you."

"Richie—"

"No. I know I'm right, and that's why I was trying to change. I want you to want me. I want you to want to be with me."

"And I do. You don't have to dress this way for me to want that."

"You don't understand. You're perfect for me. You're much better than Francis ever was, and there's a reason for that. It's the same reason I should be good for you."

Gilbert looked lost and confused. "What are you trying to tell me?"

Richie sucked in a breath. He hadn't thought he'd ever do this, but Gilbert deserved to know. He deserved to understand how messed up Richie was, how even though he should be perfect for Gilbert, he was far from it. Maybe Francis had broken him, and now, he and Gilbert couldn't fit together.

"We're mates," Richie said. "You're my mate, Gilbert. I'm so sorry."

Gilbert wasn't sure what to focus on first. He'd wanted to know why Richie was behaving this way, and now he did. The problem was that it didn't help him know how to behave.

He decided to go with his gut feeling. The first thing he wanted to talk about was the last words Richie had told him. "Why are you sorry?"

Richie looked sad, much more so than Gilbert had ever seen him. "How can you ask that? I'm sorry because it's not fair to you. You deserve the perfect mate, and instead, you have me. I'm a mess. I should have told you we were mates when I realized, but I lied to you instead. I'm broken. I don't know how you could ever want to be with me in the state I'm in, and I don't know if I can heal."

Gilbert should have known it would be something like this. Once again, he wanted to find Francis and kick the shit out of him. Since that wouldn't help and he didn't want to see Francis ever again, he decided to focus on Richie.

"Why don't we sit down?" he said.

Richie looked around as if he didn't quite understand what Gilbert was saying. Gilbert took a chance and gently wrapped his fingers around Richie's wrist. He pulled, keeping the contact gentle, and Richie came.

Gilbert guided them to sit on the porch steps. They could have used the chairs on the porch, but he thought this gave them a bit more distance from the house. They sat side by side, and Gilbert gave both of them a moment to think about what had just happened. He knew he would have to be honest and open with Richie, and he was ready for it.

He'd never imagined he was Richie's mate. He'd never imagined he had a mate at all. He was human, and he'd watched the Long brothers meet their mates one after the other. Jack and Andy were the only ones who hadn't, but Gilbert suspected it wouldn't be long before it was their turn.

But right now, it was his. Being Richie's mate meant he

truly was part of Richie's family, which was a whole other thing to think about. For now, it would be better to focus on Richie.

"When did you realize?" he asked.

Richie didn't look at him when he answered. "The day I came back. When Laurie handed you Melissa, and you had to lean over me to take her."

Now that Gilbert thought about it, he remembered that Richie had looked shocked. Gilbert had thought it had to do with Francis and what Richie had gone through, so he hadn't given it too much thought. "You didn't tell me."

"I'm sorry about that. I wanted to tell you, and I thought you should know, but I was afraid."

That made sense, too. After what Richie had gone through with Francis, he wouldn't want anyone to have any kind of power over him. From what Gilbert knew about shifters, they'd do anything to be with their mates. It gave their mates some kind of power over them, which was exactly what Richie had been trying to avoid. Besides, even without the bond, there was no way Richie was ready for a relationship.

But he'd talked to Laurie. He'd tried to make himself into a man Gilbert would want to date. What did that mean?

"I don't mind that you didn't tell me," Gilbert said. "I understand why you didn't, and I never want you to be uncomfortable or afraid of me."

Richie looked at his hands, which were clutching his knees. "You deserve to be with someone better than me. It's not fair that you have to deal with all my problems."

"But isn't that what mates are? Actually, never mind mates. Two people in a relationship shouldn't have a problem dealing with the other's problems. That's the point of being in one, isn't it?"

"Maybe. It's still not fair to you."

"I don't care about fair. I care about you." Gilbert

swallowed. He was afraid to put himself out there and get hurt, but he couldn't avoid doing that in this situation. It was more important to make sure Richie was okay and felt safe. "I don't mind waiting as long as you need me to. I don't mind keeping my distance and allowing you to do things at your pace. I know what you've been through, and I understand this isn't going to be easy. And before you say it's not fair, I don't care. The way I see things, finding out I'm your mate makes up for all of that."

"What do you mean?" Richie whispered.

"I've watched your brothers meeting their mates and falling in love with them. I mean, I never thought I'd see the day when Laurie willingly decided to have a relationship with someone. Yet, with Alexis, he's different than I've ever seen him with anyone else."

"Because Alexis is his mate."

"Right. He makes Laurie happier than anyone else ever could. It's not only that Laurie wants to be in a relationship with him. It's also in the way Laurie looks at him. It's in how they complete each other. Laurie has changed since he met Alexis, although part of that has to do with Melissa. But he's more settled and happier. He's never had that with anyone else, and I don't think he could have. Alexis is special to him, and they're happy together. I want that kind of relationship, too."

Gilbert had been watching the brothers, but also Richie's parents. He'd never thought he could have this, and now that there was a possibility he could, he'd do everything possible to keep it.

"I don't know if I can give it to you. You know about my problems. You know about Francis."

"So it won't be easy. What relationship is? This is something both of us will have to deal with, just like Laurie and Alexis had to deal with Melissa. I think that as long as we both agree we really want to give this a try, we can do it."

"What if it's too hard?"

Gilbert had to take a chance again. He reached out, gently taking Richie's hand into his. When he linked their fingers together, he felt Richie tense, but he kept his hold loose, and Richie eventually relaxed. "Are you uncomfortable right now?" he asked.

"Of course not." Richie's answer was too quick and obviously a lie.

"I know you are, and I don't want you to lie to me. You're doing it because you think I won't take it well, aren't you?"

Richie hesitated, then nodded. "I don't know how not to do that. I learned to keep Francis happy as much as I could, which meant going along with everything he wanted. My instinct is to do the same with you."

"And that's why we have to talk to each other and be honest. I'm not like Francis, and I know you're aware of that. The problem is that your instincts tell you to act as if I were. I want you to tell me when I do something that makes you uncomfortable. When it happens, we can work together to change that, either by me stopping what I'm doing or by you working through it. You're not alone. No matter what your fear tells you, I'm not going to start hitting you. I want you to be happy, and that's not going to happen if you're afraid of me."

"I know all of that," Richie quietly said. "It's just that sometimes, it's hard to keep it in mind. Fear takes over and makes me react even when I don't want to."

"And that's okay. I don't expect anything from you but honesty. Even if in the end, you decide this is too much and you're not ready for it, and you might never be, I'll be okay with it."

"It still doesn't feel fair," Richie murmured.

"Then I don't care about fairness. I only care about you and your happiness."

It was strange considering how little they knew each other, but Gilbert truly felt that way. Hopefully, Richie would realize that. If he didn't, well, Gilbert would keep telling him until he did.

CHAPTER FIVE

"Is your boyfriend coming?" Jack teased.

Richie rolled his eyes. That was the only answer his brother deserved, but it didn't deter Jack from pushing.

"Come on, tell me. You know, I always thought Gilbert was cute."

That got Richie's attention. He glared at his brother, wondering if Jack would try to steal Gilbert away from him. It was a ridiculous thought, and not just because Gilbert wasn't a thing to be stolen. Jack was only teasing, and Gilbert wasn't interested in anyone but Richie, no matter how hard that was to accept. Richie still wasn't sure he did. He didn't want Richie just because they were mates, since he was human and couldn't feel the bond between them. Yet he was still there. There had to be more to it, and Richie was still trying to puzzle it out.

Jack grinned wickedly. "What? I have eyes. Everyone in this house does, but the only ones who can still do something about it are me and Andy."

"And you don't want to do anything about it," Gilbert's father said as he walked behind the couch. "If you do, I won't hesitate to put you over my knee and spank you."

Jack grimaced. "You're not the kind of daddy I want."

Their father made a strangled sound, but Richie found himself laughing.

God, he'd missed this. He hadn't realized how much he was losing when Francis had forbidden him to visit his family, but now that he had them back, he did. Jack was inappropriate in the best of ways, especially when he was teasing.

Richie realized his father and his brother were staring at him. Once he stopped laughing, he asked, "What?"

"What were you laughing about?" Jack asked.

"Dad's face when you called him daddy. Come on. The three of us know what you were referring to, which, by the way, how do *you* know that?" Richie asked, turning toward his father.

The man crossed his arms over his chest. "I might be your father, but it doesn't mean I don't have a sex life."

Richie didn't want to hear about this any more than Jack, but he was enjoying himself too much. "Really? I wouldn't have thought you and Mom had time anymore, what with seven children."

"Well, all of you are adults." Richie's father winked at him and leaned his hip against the couch. "We've been experimenting lately, and your mother got me some books."

Jack made a retching sound and shot to his feet. "This is horrible. I hate you," he told their father. He turned toward Richie, pointing a finger at his face. "And you. I hate you, too."

He ran out of the room, leaving Richie laughing so hard his stomach hurt. His father moved from his spot against the back of the couch and took Jack's place next to Richie. He cupped a hand on the back of Richie's neck, and when the panic threatened to rise, Richie pushed it down. This was his father, not Francis. His dad would never hurt him, and he loved him. It was real love, not the kind of love Francis had used against Richie. Still, Richie was glad when his father limited himself to squeezing the back of his neck and let go.

"It's good to hear you laugh," his dad murmured.

Richie found himself smiling. "It's good to laugh. Once, I wasn't sure I'd ever laugh again."

Richie knew his father wanted to talk about Francis, but he was done beating that dead horse. What Francis had done to him was in the past, and talking about it and giving details wasn't going to change anything. Richie didn't want to give his ex any more of his time. It was bad enough that because of Francis, he was afraid of shadows.

"I'm glad you came home to us when you needed us," his father said. "I know it hasn't been easy for you, and I've tried giving you space, but I want you to know that whatever happens, whatever you need, your mother and I will always be there for you. The same goes for your brothers."

Francis had almost ruined that for Richie. If he'd had things his way, Richie would never have seen his parents again. He probably wouldn't have even realized he missed them, because Francis had occupied all his mental space.

Yet even though he hadn't talked to them in so long, even though he'd stayed away for more than a year, they'd welcomed him back. He would never forget that, because he would never allow himself to forget it. This was what love was. It was what his family was. Whatever Richie and Francis had, it was nothing like this.

Richie had been back home for close to two months now. He was getting antsy, and for once, it had nothing to do with Francis. Richie had given himself time to heal, but it was time to move forward. His first step into a new life had been telling Gilbert they were mates. He'd allowed Gilbert into his life, and they'd been dating, or at least Richie thought they were. He didn't have a lot of experience, but the fact that he and Gilbert hadn't even kissed made him wonder. His father probably wasn't the best person to ask about this, or maybe he was. Asking him meant Richie wouldn't be made fun of like he might be if he asked one of his brothers.

He swallowed. "Can I ask you a question?"

His father looked surprised, but he nodded. "Of course."

76

"You know Gilbert and I have been spending time together."

"I do. I'm glad you like him. He's a good kid."

"He is." Richie wasn't even bothered by the age difference. It was only seven years, and Gilbert had needed to grow up fast after his mother had died. "We had a good conversation a few weeks ago, outside the kitchen. I told him I wanted to be with him, and he agreed. The problem is, I'm not sure we're dating."

Richie's father frowned. "What do you mean? You're always going out with him."

"But is it dating? I mean, we haven't even kissed."

The only serious relationship, the only real dating Richie had done, had been with Francis. Before Francis, Richie had stuck to one-night stands and friends with benefits. There had been no dating, which he suspected was one of the reasons Francis had been able to sweep him off his feet the way he had. He'd made Richie feel things he'd never felt before, and he'd fallen for him quickly. By the time he realized Francis didn't care about him, it had been too late.

But Gilbert did care about Richie. Richie was sure of that, which was why he wanted so much more with him. Gilbert was his mate. And now, after watching his brothers being with their mates, Richie yearned for what they had. He just wasn't sure how to go about it.

"Have you talked to Gilbert about this?" Richie's father asked.

"Not yet. I already know what he'd say, though."

For some reason, that made Richie's father smile. "Do you? What do you think he'd say, then?"

"That what we do or don't do doesn't matter as long as we're both comfortable with it. That we don't have to do what everyone else is doing."

"And you don't think he's right."

"I know he is. I just think I'm ready for more, but I don't know what to do about it."

"Well, it's been a while since I dated anyone."

That made Richie laugh. "About forty years."

"Exactly. But considering how long I've been with your mother, I think I can give you advice. Talk to Gilbert. Tell him what you want. Especially considering what happened to you, I think it's the best thing you can do."

He was right. It would be too easy for Richie to overthink things or even to misunderstand them. Sometimes, he still looked at what Gilbert did with Francis in mind, and it wasn't fair to Gilbert. He was nothing like Francis, and while Richie was convinced of that, sometimes, it wasn't easy to remember it.

He was afraid. There was no denying that, and it wouldn't stop anytime soon. But Richie had come to terms with it. Those were his fears, and Gilbert had nothing to do with them. It wasn't fair to hold them against him.

He sighed. "I don't like talking about feelings." Because he'd been forced to hide what he felt for three years.

His father patted his knee. "I know. But if you want a successful relationship with Gilbert, you're going to have to accept that you have to. It's the only way to work things through."

Sometimes, Richie wished his father didn't make so much sense.

A quick knock on the door and the sound of it opening made Richie turn toward the entrance. He grinned, which in turn, made his father smile.

"Your boyfriend is here," his father teased.

Richie got to his feet. His boyfriend *was* here, and he intended to take advantage of every single minute he could spend with Gilbert.

Gilbert was smiling as he walked into the Long's house. He always was when he came around, but especially so since he and Richie had started dating. He couldn't wait to see his mate, and his smile widened when Richie appeared in the living room door.

They smiled at each other like idiots. Gilbert moved closer, taking Richie's hand and kissing him on the cheek. "How are you doing?" he asked.

"I'm fine. What about you?"

Someone made a retching sound. Gilbert didn't have to look to know who it was—Jack. He was the worst offender when it came to teasing, but Gilbert could tell it was always in good fun. He wouldn't be teasing Richie right now if he didn't think Richie could stand it. It was a sign of how much he loved his brother, and while Gilbert didn't fully understand, he was happy the brothers had this. It made him wish he had brothers, too, but he supposed he did now.

"It's an epidemic," Jack declared as he walked into the entrance.

Richie hooked an arm around Gilbert's shoulders. He'd been doing things like that more often, and every time, Gilbert's heart started racing. They were taking things slow, but it was more than enough for him. As long as Richie was comfortable and happy, he was, too.

"What's an epidemic?" Richie asked.

"All of you finding people to date. Well, the others found their mates, but you know what I mean."

Richie and Gilbert looked at each other. They hadn't yet told anyone they were mates, but maybe it was time. Gilbert wouldn't do it without Richie approving of it, so it was better if Richie did it.

Jack sucked in an audible breath. "What's this about? What aren't the two of you telling me?"

Richie turned back to his brother. "Why do you think we're hiding something?"

"It's in the way you look at each other. I can tell. I've been watching the others with their mates, and they share the same looks."

"You've been watching us? Should I be worried?"

Jack's eyes narrowed. "Don't try to change the topic of this conversation."

"I'm not. I'm just wondering why you've been watching your brothers and their mates. It sounds kind of stalkerish. Or maybe you're jealous? Maybe you want a boyfriend, too," Richie teased.

Jack crossed his arms over his chest. "I'm fine on my own."

"So was Laurie, yet here he is, having found his mate."

And gained a daughter, but Gilbert didn't add that. Jack was one of the brothers who was more uncomfortable with the baby, although Gilbert knew it had more to do with Melissa being a baby rather than the fact that she was Laurie's daughter.

"I won't give in the way he did," Jack declared.

"What if you meet your mate? Because Laurie didn't want a boyfriend, and technically, he doesn't have one. He has a mate, and that's different from having a boyfriend."

"Why are we talking about me right now? I was talking about *you*."

"Were we? I don't remember."

With that, Richie grabbed Gilbert's hand and pulled him deeper into the house. Jack protested and came after them. They walked into the kitchen, and Gilbert's smile widened.

The entire family was gathered there. The back door was open, and he could see Manuel and Leon sitting on the porch steps, their heads close together as they talked. They both looked up when Jack started loudly protesting that Richie and Gilbert were hiding something, and they scrambled to their feet, eager to hear.

Gilbert wasn't surprised. He'd gotten to know them since they'd entered the family, and he liked them. He liked everyone here, Marie and Richard, the brothers, and the mates.

"What's going on?" Manuel asked as he walked into the house.

Jack pointed at Richie and Gilbert. "They're hiding something."

"And that's your business why?" Laurie asked as he placed Melissa into Richie's arms.

Richie had to let go of Gilbert's hand to take the child, but Gilbert didn't mind. Richie was fascinated by the baby, and probably by the fact that she was his baby brother's daughter. He'd been far from his family for so long that it had to feel strange but also good.

Melissa immediately grabbed one of Richie's fingers and tried to put it in her mouth. Richie chuckled, and Gilbert's heart felt like it was about to explode.

"It's my business because they're family. I want to know what's going on," Jack said

Gilbert arched a brow at Jack's words. "Are you going to start stomping like a child? Is this a temper tantrum?"

"It started when I said everyone was with their mates except for Richie," Jack continued, not paying attention to Gilbert.

"That's enough," his mother intervened.

Jack looked like he wanted to protest, but he knew better. Everyone did.

Marie nodded. "If Richie and Gilbert have something to tell us, they will, in their own time. So stop sticking your nose in their business and help me set the table."

Jack pouted, but he took the stack of plates she held out and disappeared into the dining room.

Marie turned to smile at Gilbert. "That won't keep him

away for long, but for now, he should leave you alone."

"Thank you," Richie said.

"You look good with a child in your arms," his mother said.

Richie's eyes widened. "Gilbert and I aren't having a kid," he blurted out.

Marie laughed. "I know you're not. I was just saying you look good with her in your arms. Gilbert is too young to become a father."

Gilbert snorted. "Laurie's the same age I am."

"And he knows he made a mistake," Marie said, her tone uncompromising. She looked at her other sons, who were gathered around the breakfast table. "But my other children *are* old enough to become parents. When are *you* giving me grandkids?"

Suddenly, everyone seemed to have something to do outside of the kitchen. Marie wasn't easily deterred. "Curtis?" she asked.

Curtis froze, looking like a deer in headlights. "Yes?"

"Have you and Manuel talked about having children?"

Curtis and Manuel looked at each other. "No?" Curtis said, making it sound like a question.

"What are you waiting for? You're not that young anymore, Curtis."

Curtis sputtered. "I'm only thirty-three. The twins are older than me by three years."

"And they should start thinking about children, too. Do you want to wait until you're too old to play with them?"

"What's happening right now?" Leon whispered.

Gilbert grinned. "You should sneak out before she turns her attention to you. You're dating one of the twins, after all."

And while Marie would probably leave Peter, Sean's mate, alone because of how shy and quiet he was, she wouldn't hesitate to pepper Leon with questions. He could stand on his own with her and the brothers.

Leon snorted. "I'm too high maintenance to have kids," he declared.

That turned Marie's attention to him. "So you and Hugh don't want children?"

Normally, Marie wouldn't have pushed to get answers to that question. She loved her children, and she didn't expect any of them to have kids if they didn't want to. But she'd effectively turned everyone's attention away from Richie and toward this topic, and she'd done it on purpose. Gilbert was sure of that.

The brothers loved Richie, and now that Richie had been home for a few months, they treated him the way they did each other. That was a good thing, because it helped Richie not obsess over what Francis had done, but it also meant that sometimes, it was too much.

Gilbert moved closer to Richie. "I love your mom," he said.

Richie beamed. "I love her, too. And look. Jack hasn't returned yet."

Gilbert doubted he would. He was scared of his mother.

"Richie!" a voice yelled.

All of them froze. Richie's eyes went wide, and he was turned to stare out the window that opened toward the front of the house. Gilbert didn't have to look to know who was there, calling for Richie. Richie's reaction was enough, and he recognized the voice.

"Francis is here," he said.

Richie couldn't move. He wasn't surprised that Francis was here, but he was done with his ex.

He'd been home for two months, and Francis hadn't come for him. Richie had believed it meant Francis had enough and was turning his attention to someone else, but he should have known better. Francis liked control, and he'd lost the control he had over Richie. He wanted it back, and apparently, he was ready to face Richie's entire family to make that happen.

This was going to be a mess. Now that Gilbert had told everyone in the room who was calling Richie, Richie could see his brothers were gearing up for a fight. As was his mother, for that matter, and Richie wouldn't be surprised if she was the one to strike Francis first. His mother had never been violent, but Francis had hurt one of her sons. It meant a lot to her.

He quickly thrust Melissa back into Laurie's arms. Laurie looked like he wanted to protest, but she was his daughter, so he didn't. Once Richie was sure she was safe, he rushed toward the front door. He hoped to get there before his brothers. But with so many of them in the same room, trying to do the same, they got stuck. By the time Richie finally reached the entrance, Jack had already opened the front door and was standing on the porch, his arms crossed over his chest, glaring at Francis.

It was a miracle Jack hadn't hit him yet, and Richie hoped that would continue.

Richie hadn't seen Francis in two months, but the man hadn't changed. He was still bulging with muscles, which had always scared Richie. Richie had to remember he wasn't alone anymore. He had the support of his family, and he had his mate. Whatever Francis did or said, Richie had gotten away from him once. He could do it again, but he didn't think he'd have to because he was never going back to Francis.

Richie looked around. Jack was still on the porch, but he wasn't the only one. Richie's parents were there, too, along with all of Richie's brothers except for Laurie, who was standing just inside the door, glaring at Francis while holding Melissa. Even the mates were there. Leon looked like he wanted to tear Francis's eyes out, and Manuel was holding on to him. Peter was at the back of the group, looking terrified, but it touched Richie to know he was there, even though he was afraid. Alexis was standing with Laurie, ready to take Melissa if he had to.

Richie was surrounded by his family.

Francis seemed to understand the mistake he'd made by coming here. He no doubt hadn't realized they were having a family dinner, even after he'd seen the cars parked along the driveway and the sidewalk. He paled, but Richie knew him. That wouldn't be enough for him to step back.

Just like Richie had expected, Francis took a step forward rather than back. "I'm taking you home," he said.

"He already *is* home," Jack answered.

Marie put a hand on Jack's arm and shook her head. Jack opened his mouth to protest, but she leaned closer and whispered something to him. Jack didn't look happy, but he nodded at her and, surprisingly, stayed where he was instead of jumping off the porch and beating Francis into the ground.

Richie's family was here to protect him if he needed them. They were there to support him so he knew he wasn't alone. But they were also allowing him to do this by himself. They knew he needed it, and while it was petrifying, he could do it.

He had to.

"Why should I go with you?" he asked. He was proud of the fact that his voice only trembled a little.

"Come on, baby. I know you love me. I'm ready to forgive what you did and take you back. We can be happy again."

Richie's stomach churned. This was the voice Francis had used to convince him to stay time and time again. Each time Richie gave in, Francis made sure he couldn't run away. Then he hit him. Richie had no doubt that was what would happen if he went with Francis right now. He'd probably be good until they were back at the apartment, but it would end there. As soon as he had Richie cornered, he'd make sure Richie didn't even *think* about leaving again.

"I don't love you," Richie declared. "I don't think I ever did." What he'd felt for Francis didn't come close to what he felt for Gilbert. He might have been infatuated in the beginning, but Francis himself had made sure Richie didn't fall for him, no matter what Richie had thought.

Francis's expression grew rageful.

Richie knew he wanted to come closer and hit him, but thankfully, he stayed where he was. "We've been together for three years. You can't throw that away for nothing," Francis tried.

"We were together because I was afraid of you. You abused me, but that's over. I left, and I'm never coming back."

"Who made you think those things? I never abused you. I love you, and I'd never hurt someone I love."

Richie raised his hand to touch his lip. It had healed, but sometimes, he felt like it still hurt. "What do you call hitting me because I wanted a haircut?"

Francis looked away from Richie and toward the brothers. "A misunderstanding. You know I like your hair longer." His focus moved back to Richie, and Richie knew Francis was looking at his hair. "I see you cut it anyway. That's fine. It'll grow back."

Richie couldn't believe what he was hearing, or rather, he could, because this was Francis. He was great at bullshitting his way through life, and in any other situation, Richie would have probably gone back to him. He'd have been too scared not to.

But no matter how scared he was now, he was never going back. Coming home, meeting Gilbert, all of that had shown him how strong he was. Or maybe he hadn't been strong before, but he was now. It felt that way, and he'd needed this new strength to face Francis.

He took a step forward, then another. He started walking

down the porch steps, and Francis's expression turned to triumph. He thought he'd won, which was what Richie wanted.

Jack called out to Richie, but Richie didn't turn around to look at him. He knew what he was doing, or at least, he hoped so.

He didn't stop moving until he was in front of Francis. He had to swallow because Francis had always been bigger than him, but it seemed to have gotten worse over the few months they hadn't seen each other. How could someone be so big? It couldn't be natural, even though Francis was a shifter.

Richie was still afraid of him, but he'd come to realize it wasn't a bad thing. He didn't have to conquer his fears. He had to accept them and the fact that they were part of him. Then, he had to ignore them.

"I'm never going back to you," he said. He was pleased that his voice was strong and steady. "You're an abusive piece of shit. I should have realized that sooner, and when I did, I should have left your ass. I didn't because I was afraid of you, and I still am. But I'm not alone anymore. Even if I were, I wouldn't allow you to touch me again. I'd rather die."

Francis opened his mouth, but Richie wasn't done.

"I know. You'll forgive me if I stop talking back to you and do what you want. That's what you say now, but we both know you'll have to *punish* me since I cut my hair and I'm wearing clothes you don't like, and of course, because I left you. You just want me to leave my family so you'll have the freedom to do all of that. I'm not falling for it again. The decision to leave you was the best I've ever made, and I'm not going back on it."

Never again.

Gilbert was so fucking proud of Richie that he felt like his chest might burst.

He was sure none of them had expected Richie to face Francis. They'd been ready to jump in and save Richie, but Richie hadn't needed them to. He hadn't last time, either. He was much stronger than he gave himself credit for, and Gilbert would make sure to remind him of that time and time again.

Francis's face was so red that Gilbert wondered if it might explode. He obviously had never had anyone push back against him the way Richie was. He'd come here thinking he'd drag Richie back to his apartment easily, but instead, he was faced with all the brothers, their mates, and Richie's parents. No matter what happened next, they'd make sure Francis could never hurt Richie again.

Instead of accepting that he'd been defeated, Francis glared at Richie. "What do you think you're doing? I was good to you for three years. Even when I could have dumped you, I stayed with you. Who do you think is going to take you now? You're so weak and pathetic that no one but me will want you."

Gilbert couldn't help it—he snorted. Apparently, the sound was loud enough for Francis to hear him, because he turned toward him. Gilbert wasn't ashamed of the fact that he was with Richie. Why would he be? Francis had used his power and words to make Richie feel weak. However, there was nothing further from the truth, and Richie knew it now. Gilbert was proud to be with him and to be his mate, and he wouldn't hesitate to say it to Francis's face.

Apparently, he wouldn't have to. The snort had been enough for Francis to understand that Richie and Gilbert were together, and when he looked back to Richie, fury distorted his face. "You're sleeping with that guy?" he asked.

Richie didn't have to look to know who Francis was talking about. "If you're talking about the cute guy at the front, yes, we're together. So, you see, I won't need you anymore. I already have another boyfriend, and he's much nicer than you.

He's also better in bed."

Gilbert almost laughed. Richie wouldn't know if that was true because they hadn't slept together yet, but he didn't mind Richie saying it. It was worth it to see Francis's expression.

"You slut," Francis ground out. He pulled a fist back, intent on punching Richie.

Gilbert sucked in a breath. The brothers were already moving, intent on saving Richie from the beating. They didn't have to because before they could reach Richie and Francis, Richie hit Francis with a punch. It landed on his left cheek, and while it wasn't enough to throw him to the ground, he looked shocked that Richie would do something like that.

Richie grimaced and shook his hand. "Dammit. Are you made of rocks?" he asked.

Francis's cheek was red, and Gilbert felt a savage satisfaction at the thought that he'd be bruised. He didn't normally enjoy violence, but it was good to see someone do to him what he usually did to others.

Richie's brothers had stopped moving. They were ready to act if Francis tried to retaliate, but thankfully — or maybe unfortunately, because Gilbert wouldn't have minded seeing him beaten to a pulp — he wasn't that stupid.

He took a step back. He was glaring at everyone, but especially at Richie. He pointed a finger at him. "You'll regret this."

"I don't think so. You think you're a catch, but admit it, at least to yourself. You're not. You use violence and abuse to force people to stay with you. What kind of man does that make you? I wouldn't come back to you even if you were the last man on earth. I don't care if I'm alone for the rest of my life. I never want to see you again."

Francis took a step forward again, reaching for Richie. This time, Richie didn't have to punch him. Before anything could happen, Jack screamed and rushed toward Francis. Gilbert's eyes widened when he saw that Jack had grabbed the broom his mother kept on the porch and was holding it high above his head, obviously intent on using it on Francis.

Francis ran away so fast it surprised Gilbert. How could such a big man move so quickly?

Jack went after him, and he wasn't the only one. Andy was right behind him, although he was empty-handed, as were the others. Curtis and Leon almost fell on their faces when their paths crossed as they ran. Sean ran past them, his focus entirely on Francis, who had opened his truck and was scrambling into it.

Richie stayed where he was, and Gilbert went to him. Richie jerked away when he felt him, but he relaxed when he saw who it was. He wrapped an arm around Gilbert's shoulders while Gilbert hooked one around Richie's waist. Together, they watched as Francis tried to drive away. He was having a bit of a problem because Leon had grabbed the handle of the door on Francis's side and was trying to pry it open, cursing like a sailor as he did so.

"I should probably grab my mate," Hugh said.

Gilbert didn't know why he found it so funny, but he started laughing. Richie looked at him and burst out laughing, too. Their shoulders shook, and they had to lean against each other not to fall. For all that they were scaring Francis, Gilbert doubted any of the brothers would hurt him. Well, Jack and Leon might, but not the others. They were making a show so Francis knew never to come back, and Gilbert thought it would be a success.

Hugh walked to the truck, grabbed Leon around the waist, and hauled him away. Leon protested and tried to get to Francis again, but his mate wasn't letting go. Now that the truck was free, Francis gunned it out of there. He didn't even look back at Richie.

"You think we'll see him again?" he asked Richie.

Richie shook his head. "He thinks he's strong until someone punches back. I've seen it happen several times, so I'm not surprised he ran away when my brothers went after him. He knows they'll be waiting for him if he tries coming back into my life, but also that I won't hesitate to punch him if I have to. I might lose because of how much stronger he is, but it doesn't matter. The control he had over me is broken, so he won't want me anymore."

Gilbert suspected he was right. "I'm proud of you."

Richie smiled. "I'm proud of myself, too. I never thought I'd be so brave, but thanks to you and my family, I am."

"It's not thanks to us. You were always brave. You just had to believe in yourself."

Richie turned around so they faced each other. Gilbert wasn't surprised when Richie cupped his face with both his hands and leaned down to kiss him. He'd been waiting for this since they'd had the talk on the back porch, but even then, his heart raced.

Richie brushed their lips together. Gilbert stayed still, not wanting to push Richie too far. Whatever Richie wanted, Gilbert would give him.

What Richie wanted was another kiss. After the first brush of their lips, he leaned down again, and Gilbert could feel he was smiling. The kiss was deeper this time, their tongues hesitantly touching each other as they learned how the other tasted.

"You should have let me beat him," Leon said from somewhere behind them.

Gilbert started laughing. How could he not? Francis had been bigger even than Richie, but he'd positively dwarfed Leon.

Richie laughed with him. When they turned around, the entire family was looking at them. Richie twined his fingers with Gilbert's. "Jack was right."

It took a moment for Jack to understand. When he did, he pointed at them. "So the two of you *are* mates?"

Richie nodded. "I found out the day I came back, but we decided to take things slow."

"I don't care about any of that. I just care that I was right," Jack crowed.

Gilbert laughed again. These people might not be related to him by blood, but they were family anyway, and he was glad he'd found them.

He was even happier he'd found Richie.

CHAPTER SIX

Richie was still afraid. It was a month since Francis had come to drag him home, but Richie still looked around when he was in public to make sure his ex wasn't there. It would take time to stop doing that, but he couldn't wait for it to happen. As it was, it felt like Francis still had a hold on him, and Richie didn't like it. Unfortunately, there was little he could do about it, and he'd made his peace with that.

He'd made his peace with a lot of things. He was proud of himself, both for kicking Francis out of his life and for the step he was taking today.

He was looking at apartments.

He'd started working with Sean. He didn't know a lot about construction work, but he'd worked with his father when he was younger, like all his brothers. What he knew was enough for Sean, and Richie was surprised at how much he enjoyed working with his brother. It wasn't his dream job, but then he couldn't remember ever having one of those.

He didn't know what he'd do next with his life. Maybe he'd continue working for Sean. Maybe eventually he'd find something else. It didn't matter.

The job with Sean earned Richie enough money to get his own apartment, which was what he was trying to do. It would be a little longer until he got a car. But Jack had already promised he'd keep an eye out for one, and as a mechanic, it wouldn't be a problem even if the car wasn't in great shape. Jack could fix it, and he seemed intent on doing just that.

"What do you think?" Gilbert asked.

He was standing in the middle of the living room, slowly turning around to look at everything. Richie had wanted him to come along, and he was glad Gilbert had agreed. Still, there was something wrong, and Richie couldn't quite place his finger on it.

"I don't know," he said slowly.

Gilbert didn't look angry, even though it was the second apartment Richie didn't like today. "Do you think you know what's wrong with it? That way, we can make sure it doesn't happen during the next visit."

"It's small."

Gilbert chuckled. "Well, it's an apartment. I understand wanting more, but unless you want a roommate, you probably won't be able to afford anything else."

Richie was aware of that, and he knew it was all in his head. He should take this apartment because he could afford it and it wasn't far from his parents' house. He needed to stop hesitating so much, but it wasn't easy.

It wasn't just because of the apartments not being what he wanted. Even though Richie knew he should live by himself, he was scared. He didn't know if he could do it. His parents had been there for him when he'd needed them, and they were his support system. Could he do this on his own?

Francis had always told him how stupid and unable to survive on his own he was. He'd believed it for a long time, and sometimes, he still did. He knew it was Francis talking in his mind, but that didn't make it easier to ignore. That fear wasn't one he could just push away. In Gilbert's case, Richie could look at how Gilbert behaved to know that Gilbert was different from Francis and that he wouldn't hurt him. In this situation, though, how was Richie supposed to believe he could be on his own?

Gilbert moved closer and gently took one of Richie's hands. Richie's first instinct was still to cringe away, but he forced himself to stay where he was. Gilbert wouldn't hurt him, and if Richie wanted a real relationship with him, he had to stop acting like an idiot.

"What is it?" Gilbert asked.

"What if I can't do it?"

Gilbert didn't tell him he was stupid. He didn't ask what Richie meant. "But what if you can? I know you want to be independent, and I understand. Your family does, too. They want you to be happy, and you won't be if you stay with your parents for much longer. Moving out doesn't mean you're going to lose them."

"I know I won't. I'm just not sure I can do this on my own."

"Did you before?"

Before Francis, Richie had lived on his own. He'd been doing well, or at least, he thought he had. "For a few years," he confirmed.

"Then it probably won't be a problem, especially after the first few weeks. You should have more faith in yourself."

"I want to." But he didn't want to be on his own.

He wanted to be with Gilbert.

Maybe that was only a way for Richie not to be on his own, but maybe it wasn't.

Gilbert kissed Richie's hand, then let it go and stepped away. Richie didn't stop him, needing some time to think.

He wanted to move in with Gilbert. He wanted a bigger house, something that could become a true home for him. He wouldn't even mind a fixer-upper, because he knew Sean would help him fix it the way he wanted it.

But he couldn't afford something like that on his own. He had a bit of money—his parents had insisted he accept his part of the inheritance from his grandparents since he needed it—so he could probably afford a down payment, especially if the house needed fixing. But what about everything else? Fixing the house would take money, as would paying the mortgage.

So Richie wanted to move in with Gilbert because he wanted a bigger house, and he wanted to buy it. Was that the only reason?

It wasn't. Richie was in love with Gilbert, and they were mates. He wanted a lengthy relationship with Gilbert, and now that they were dating, the next step could be moving in together. Gilbert probably wouldn't say no if Richie asked to move into his apartment, but it was tiny. What would Gilbert think of both of them moving into a house?

Richie licked his lips. Thinking about Gilbert possibly rejecting him was terrifying, but if he wanted to know for sure, he'd have to ask.

"Richie?" Gilbert asked gently.

Richie swallowed. "I don't hate this place, but I don't think it's for me," he said.

Gilbert nodded as if he'd expected it. He probably had. "All right. We can go and see more apartments next week."

"What if I don't want to see more apartments?"

Gilbert frowned. "I know you want a house, but I doubt you can afford it."

"I can't. I'd like to find a fixer-upper, but even then, it's too much money for me." Richie hesitated, then decided he might as well say it. What was the worst that could happen? Gilbert might say no, and it would hurt, but Richie would understand. They hadn't been together long, and God knew he had a lot of baggage they both had to deal with. "It would be doable if we both moved into that house, though."

Gilbert stared. His eyes were wide, and he was gaping, which didn't tell Richie anything. He needed Gilbert to say the words, and he knew which words he wanted to hear.

Would Gilbert say them? Richie didn't know, but he did know that even if Gilbert said no, he was strong enough to weather the rejection. Dealing with Francis had shown him that, and he would never allow himself to forget it.

Gilbert wasn't sure what to say. He hadn't expected Richie to want them to live together, not so soon. His first instinct was to say yes, but he was wondering if Richie had thought this through.

"You want us to move in together," he said slowly.

Richie nodded. He didn't look as hopeful as he had before.

Gilbert wondered if he'd realized he'd come too far, too quickly.

"Wouldn't it be for the best?" Richie asked. "We're going to move in together eventually anyway. We're mates."

"I'm aware, but nothing says we have to move in together now."

Richie looked away. "You don't have to say yes if you don't want to."

"I do want to." It was so easy to imagine them living together.

Richie had said he wanted a house, and Gilbert was more than okay with that. He didn't even care that from the sound of it, they'd have to renovate the place. Richie's brothers would help, and while Gilbert didn't know the first thing about renovations, he could learn.

He and Richie could rebuild the house the way they wanted. Then they could fill it with love and a family. They could get a dog, and maybe one day have children. Gilbert was only twenty, so he wasn't quite there yet, especially not considering Richie's situation, but in the future? He wanted little Richies running around the house.

Richie looked more hopeful but not over the moon happy just yet. "So you do want us to move in together?"

"I do. I'm just wondering if you're rushing things because you think you should."

Richie crossed his arms over his chest. "What do you mean?"

This wasn't the right place to do this, not with the landlord hanging around waiting for them to make a decision. Still, it was obvious Richie needed to have this conversation, so they would. "I don't want to doubt you or the fact that you can make this kind of decision."

"Yet you are."

"Not exactly. But you said yourself that you're not sure where to go from here. Francis spent three years pushing you down and making you believe you couldn't be on your own. That's why you want to leave your parents' house, isn't it? To show yourself and everyone else that you can be independent."

Richie's expression softened. "You're right. That's what I wanted to do. I need to know that I can survive on my own."

"Then how can moving in together make that happen?"

Richie raked a hand through his hair and turned away. He looked out the window, and Gilbert moved to stand next to him. The view wasn't great since it showed the alley behind a row of shops.

"It's going to take me time to heal," Richie said slowly. "And I think that part of me will always be wounded and jumpy, especially in the beginning. I don't expect to be able to forget what Francis did to me, but I hope that in time, I'll stop seeing his shadow everywhere."

Richie turned to look at Gilbert. When he took Gilbert's hand, Gilbert didn't protest. "But it's time for me to move forward. I *want* to forget about Francis and what he did to me. And I don't think that living with you makes me any less independent than I would be if I lived on my own. You're not my parents. You're my mate, and if we do this, we'll be equal partners. I don't expect you to take care of everything in the house, not the way Francis did."

Gilbert despised being compared to Francis, but he understood that Francis was the only relationship Richie had to refer to. Gilbert didn't think of it as a relationship, but Richie did, and that was what mattered.

"What do you expect, then?" Gilbert asked.

"Well, in part, I want us to move in together so we can get a bigger place. Since I already know that eventually, we'll live together and get married, I don't see why we can't start some of that now."

Richie seemed convinced of what he was saying, and while Gilbert agreed, he didn't want to think about getting married just yet. It was too much, too soon, and it looked like Richie had given it more thought than Gilbert had.

"So yes," Richie continued. "I want us to choose a house that we both like and renovate it the way we both want it. I want us to work on it together as a couple. And once we move in, I want to contribute as much as you do. I want to pay the bills and take out the trash, to clean the bathrooms and cook."

Gilbert found himself smiling. "Are those things new for you?"

"Some of them. Francis never allowed me to make any decisions when it came to the apartment we lived in. It was his before I moved in, and I couldn't change anything. He also didn't allow me to pay the bills. I could clean and cook, and actually, those were things he *expected* me to do. I guess he wanted me to be a house husband."

The less Gilbert thought about Francis, the better he felt. Unfortunately, Francis would be part of his and Richie's life for a while. Richie felt comfortable enough to talk about him now, and Gilbert wanted to honor that. "And how did you feel about it?"

"I don't mind staying at home for a bit. I mean, everyone likes a vacation, right? But then I wanted to find a job, and I wasn't allowed to do that. I wanted to be allowed to pay bills and to be trusted with money."

"But Francis didn't trust you with money."

"I think he believed I'd take it and run away or something."

"He was a fool. You didn't need money to run away." When Richie had arrived at his parents' house, he hadn't owned anything but the clothes on his back and his old phone.

Richie smiled. "I didn't, no. I don't want to talk about Francis anymore. I want to talk about us and our future. I realize it's going to take me a while to find my place in the world and with you, but I have to start somewhere. Does it make sense for me to find an apartment and live here for a few months, even a year, only for us to move in together then? Besides, if we're going to get a fixer-upper, it'll take time to renovate it. I don't think I should move into an apartment as we do so, not when I can stay with my parents. That way, I can put most of the money I earn toward the house."

"And if we do this, I'll contribute."

"Of course. The house will be ours, not mine. I'd offer for you to move in with my parents, too, but I doubt you want to."

Gilbert couldn't think of anything worse than having to deal with Richie's brothers all the time. "I'll stay at my apartment." He hesitated. "And you could move in with me. I mean, if we're going to live together in this house you keep talking about, we could start right away. We'll find out if we actually fit together." And Richie would be able to leave his parents' house, which Gilbert knew he wanted.

"The way you talk, it sounds like you're agreeing to this," Richie pointed out.

Gilbert wrapped an arm around Richie's waist. Richie barely flinched, which was an improvement. A few weeks ago, he would have been afraid Gilbert would hurt him. Gilbert wasn't offended, because he knew it was because of

Francis, not him.

But today, Richie stayed where he was. He allowed Gilbert to pull him closer, and once they were plastered against each other, he wrapped both arms around Gilbert's shoulders. He was still taller, but it felt right to stand this way.

"I do want to move in with you," Gilbert said. "I have fears, just like you do. They're not the same, but I've never lived with anyone but my father. Even when I did live with him, it was as if I was on my own. I suppose that moving into my apartment didn't change much for me, but this will. I don't know how to share a living space with someone, and I'm scared I'll make mistakes."

Richie kissed Gilbert's forehead. "You will, and so will I. And I know that with my past, we'll have to be extra careful about what we say and do. That won't change my mind, though. I want to move in with you and create a home with you."

"Then let's do it."

Richie's smile lit up the room. "Really?"

"As long as we promise each other we'll talk if there's anything wrong, yes. Let's live together."

There was nothing Gilbert wanted more, and while, like Richie had said, they would both make mistakes, Gilbert knew they'd weather anything life threw at them — together.

Richie was relieved when he and Gilbert left the apartment. They'd told the landlord they wouldn't be moving in, and while Richie was sorry it would take more time for them to find the right place, he was also happy. Now that they'd decided to move in together, they both wanted to find a house, so that was what they'd visit next time. They were done with apartments.

"What area would you like the house to be in?" Gilbert

asked as he drove. "Near your parents?"

"Would you say no if I did?"

Gilbert frowned. "Why should I?"

"A lot of guys wouldn't want to live near their in-laws."

"Well, maybe I'm not like them, because I don't mind living close to Marie and Richard. As long as they're not next door, that is."

Richie laughed. Gilbert was saying all the right things, and he was behaving the right way. They were really doing this, and while Richie still couldn't believe it, in time, he would. He had his entire life in front of him, and he'd be spending it with Gilbert. There was nothing more he wanted. Everything else would move into place as long as he had Gilbert in his life.

"Not next door, no," Richie agreed. "Not even in the next street. But close by? I'd like to be able to walk there."

"That sounds good to me. Have you noticed any houses for sale?"

"No, but we could ask Sean. Maybe he knows of some."

"Or we could get a real estate agent. I know you didn't want one when you were looking for an apartment, but this is a house, and you're planning on buying it. It's probably better if we have someone who knows what they're doing helping us."

Richie wanted to say no, that he could do this by himself, but Gilbert was right. If he'd been renting an apartment, it wouldn't have been a problem to choose it on his own. It was the house they'd both live in for the rest of their lives, though. They should have people helping them choose it, including Sean. "You're right. And I'd like to talk to Sean. I mean, he's the one who's going to help us renovate the place, so he should see the house before we buy it."

And Sean would probably *want* to see it. All of Richie's brothers were protective, even now that Francis was gone.

They tried not to show it, but Richie wasn't blind or an idiot. They sheltered him, and that was okay. He needed to be sheltered at least a bit, and there was no one better for the job than his family.

"We'll find a real estate agent," Gilbert confirmed.

Richie had been so focused on their conversation that he hadn't realized that Gilbert wasn't taking him home to his parents. Instead, he parked in front of an apartment building. When he turned to look at Richie, he appeared worried, and Richie didn't understand why until Gilbert explained where they were. "I live here. I figured that if you're going to move into my apartment for a bit, you ought to know where it is and see it."

"I'd like to see where you live," Richie confirmed.

It was a test, albeit one he was doing to himself. He and Gilbert had spent time alone, but usually, they were around town or at Richie's parents' house. Richie had never been to Gilbert's apartment, and once he was inside, no one would hear him if something happened. It meant Gilbert would have privacy to hurt him, but Richie pushed those thoughts away.

Gilbert wouldn't hurt him. He wasn't like Francis, and Richie repeated that as he and Gilbert got out of the car. He followed Gilbert inside the building and into the elevator. Gilbert was obviously nervous, as was Richie. He didn't know what to expect, but he did know Gilbert wouldn't do anything that would make him run.

"It's not much," Gilbert explained as they walked down the hallway once they'd left the elevator. "It's a one-bedroom because I couldn't afford anything else, and I didn't *need* anything else. I hope you won't mind sharing the bedroom with me."

The thought made Richie's mouth go dry. Did he want to share a bedroom with Gilbert? *Hell, yes.* Was he afraid of what would happen once they were intimate? A bit.

Sex with Francis hadn't been pleasant, not after they'd moved in together. Once again, though, that was on Francis, not on Richie. Richie was doing his best not to dump Gilbert and Francis in the same bag, but sometimes, it wasn't easy. Still, he couldn't wait to do more than kissing and the fumbling he and Gilbert had been up to recently. It felt like the next step to taking back his life—getting back the intimacy he'd missed so much over the past few years. It wasn't just about sex, although Richie did want to have sex with Gilbert. It was also about being naked together, wrapped around each other. It was about waking up with Gilbert, about lazy kisses in bed, about things Richie hadn't been allowed to have.

Now, he was.

They stopped in front of a door, and Gilbert unlocked it. He waved Richie inside, and while Richie didn't like giving Gilbert his back, he took a deep breath and stepped in.

Gilbert had been right. The apartment was nothing much, but Richie liked it. Francis's apartment had been full of modern furniture but not much else. It had looked like a hotel room more than a home, and Richie had never felt like he belonged there. Here, he did, even though technically, it wasn't his home.

There were signs of Gilbert everywhere. Framed posters hung on the walls. There was a rainbow blanket on the couch, obviously well used. The coffee table sported a mix of dirty mugs, books, and remote controls.

Gilbert's cheeks were red when he rushed toward the coffee table. Richie stopped him before he could reach it. He didn't care that the apartment was messy. If anything, he liked it.

He pulled Gilbert closer, and Gilbert stumbled. He fell against Richie, but for once, Richie wasn't afraid. He kissed Gilbert, and Gilbert's body softened against his.

This was what Richie wanted. Now that they were moving

in together, it was time to take the next step in their relationship.

Richie cupped one of Gilbert's cheeks. He kept Gilbert
there as he kissed him, but it wasn't enough. He didn't think
he'd ever get enough of Gilbert, and that was good. He'd
never felt this way, especially not with Francis.

"Where's your bedroom?" he asked.

Gilbert chuckled. "This place is tiny. You really have to
ask?"

"Well, there are two doors, and I don't know which one is
to the bedroom."

"The one on the right. The other is the bathroom."

Richie nodded. That was all he'd wanted to know, and now
that he did, he had every intention of visiting the bedroom.
They'd need the bathroom, but that would come later.

Richie was smaller than Francis, but he was bigger than
Gilbert, although not by much. Still, it was enough for him to
be able to grab Gilbert's ass and haul him into his arms. The
problem was that it didn't last long because Richie wasn't
strong enough. Gilbert squeaked and tried to wrap his legs
around Richie's waist, but Richie stumbled, and they almost
fell on their faces.

"We should probably walk there," Gilbert said.

He sounded amused, and while Richie had been trying to
be sexy, he liked this, too. Sex didn't have to be serious. It
didn't have to be in the dark, always in the same position, the
way Francis had liked it.

Richie wasn't sure how far he could push himself, but he
was sure of what he wanted.

Gilbert.

Together, they stumbled toward the bedroom. It was hard
to let go of Gilbert, so Richie didn't. He kept his arms around
his mate, even when Gilbert turned around to open his bedroom door. He held Gilbert against his body with his right

arm, and, once they were inside the bedroom, he slid his left arm around. He went straight to the point, cupping Gilbert through his jeans.

Gilbert moaned and stopped moving. He didn't tell Richie what to do or to stop, so Richie decided to explore. He had to let go of Gilbert, but Gilbert didn't move and allowed him to undo his jeans and push them down his thighs. They got stuck there, but that was okay. Maybe Richie should mention buying looser jeans for the future, though.

Richie ran his fingertips over Gilbert's cock. It was hard in his boxer briefs, long and warm. Richie kept his touch light and easy to begin with, the fabric a safe barrier between them. That didn't last long. He wanted skin, and he wanted it now.

He pushed Gilbert's boxers down his legs, too. Gilbert's cock was flushed, and, to Richie's surprise, the sight of it made his mouth water. He'd never enjoyed oral sex much, but maybe it was because he hadn't enjoyed who he had it with, not because of the act itself.

Richie wanted to try everything, but they'd have plenty of time to do that.

He turned Gilbert around and kissed him. Gilbert groaned and leaned against him, his hands going to Richie's jeans. He didn't undo them, and while Richie disliked that Gilbert was so hesitant, he understood it was necessary. Gilbert didn't want to spook him, and he didn't want that to happen, either. This was the first time he'd had sex after Francis and the first time with his mate. He wanted everything to be perfect, and while it wouldn't be, it could at least be as perfect as possible.

Gilbert tried to get closer, but he couldn't move with his jeans trapping his thighs. It made Richie laugh, and Gilbert glared at him. "It's not funny," he complained.

"I don't know about that."

Gilbert was smiling, so Richie knew he wasn't angry.

He stepped back, pulling Gilbert with him. Once they were

close enough to the bed, Richie turned them so Gilbert was under him as they dropped down. With Gilbert on his back, Richie hooked his fingers in the jeans and pulled them all the way down. He had to pause to take off Gilbert's shoes and socks, but at the same time, Gilbert got rid of his t-shirt, so once Richie was done, he was fully naked.

And what a sight he was. Richie had never seen someone so beautiful, and he didn't know where to start. He knew what he wanted, though, and since he also knew that taking too long would make him anxious and prone to overthink it, he moved quickly and took off his clothes. He looked at Gilbert the entire time to remind himself who he was with.

Before Richie could get on the bed, Gilbert gestured at the nightstand. "There's lube and condoms in there." He bit his lower lip. He looked gorgeous with his cheeks and chest flushed. "I had a chat with Laurie, and he told me we don't need to use condoms?"

Richie wasn't surprised Gilbert had talked to his brother. They were best friends, after all. "Shifters are resistant to most illnesses, so no. We can use one if it makes you more comfortable, though."

Gilbert shook his head. "No. I want to feel you."

Richie nodded. He wanted to feel Gilbert, too, but he'd have used a condom if Gilbert had wanted him to.

He opened the drawer, grabbed the lube, and sat on top of Gilbert. He straddled Gilbert's hips, which made Gilbert frown. He clearly didn't know what Richie had in mind, and maybe they should have talked about it, but it was easier to show him.

Richie opened the lube, slicked his fingers, and reached behind himself.

Gilbert's eyes widened. "You're going to . . ."

"Unless you don't do that?"

"I'm flexible. I mean, I can go either way. I just didn't think you'd want that."

Richie wasn't sure he did, but he'd always bottomed for Francis, and he wanted what he was about to do with Gilbert to replace those memories. He didn't want to fear the act, and he didn't want to be reminded of Francis every time he thought about it.

"As long as it's okay with you?" Richie asked.

Gilbert swallowed. "More than okay."

So Richie continued what he was doing. Gilbert didn't try to help, but he did run his hands over Richie's thighs and waist. Richie was grateful. Even though he knew Gilbert wouldn't hurt him, doing everything himself gave him more freedom to move away if he had to.

But he didn't.

Gilbert was allowing him to do whatever he wanted, something he hadn't had in three years.

His mouth was dry by the time he was ready and it was time to take the next step. He hesitated, but one look at Gilbert's face was enough for him to be convinced again. Gilbert wanted him as much as he wanted Gilbert. Maybe he even loved him. They hadn't said that to each other, but Richie knew how he felt, and he suspected Gilbert felt similarly.

So Richie pushed all the hesitation away, raised his hips, and moved farther up Gilbert's body. He wrapped his fingers around Gilbert's cock, which hadn't softened while Richie prepared himself. He held it up, then after taking one last deep breath, he lowered himself on top of it.

It was different. For one, Francis had always wanted to have sex in the same position, with Richie facing away from him. Maybe he didn't want Richie to look at him, although that wouldn't have mattered since he'd always turned the lights off when they did it. What Richie and Gilbert were doing was so very different, and Richie loved it.

He paused once Gilbert was fully inside of him. His thighs

already trembled, but that didn't stop him. He pressed both of his hands against Gilbert's stomach and pushed his hips up. Gilbert's cock slid out of him, but not completely. Richie pushed down again. Gilbert's cock filled him. Gilbert was everywhere, outside and inside of Richie's body — but also his mind and his heart.

Gilbert wasn't used to this. Guys usually wanted him to bottom, and he was more than happy to do it. He liked bottoming.

He also liked topping, though, and he'd do anything for Richie.

Normally, he'd be more touchy-feely, especially during sex. He wanted to touch every inch of Richie's skin, but instead, he kept his hands on Richie's thighs and waist. Richie hadn't freaked out yet, and Gilbert didn't want him to start now.

But once Richie found a rhythm, it was harder to continue not touching him. Gilbert found himself grabbing both of Richie's wrists. And when he did, Gilbert froze. He started to let go, but Richie shook his head.

"Hold them," he said.

Gilbert didn't want Richie to feel restrained, but if Richie didn't, he was ready to continue. He didn't know how sex had been between Richie and Francis. He hadn't asked, and Richie hadn't offered details. Richie knew what he was doing, though, and Gilbert was more than happy to go along with it.

Richie bounced on Gilbert's cock in a maddening rhythm. His eyes were half-closed as he looked at Gilbert, and Gilbert looked back. Since Richie hadn't had a problem with Gilbert holding his wrists, he took a chance and let go. Richie opened his mouth, but Gilbert had no intention of stopping touching him. He ran his hands over Richie's arms and chest until he reached his nipples. Once he did, he pinched them and gently pulled on them.

Richie panted, his mouth open, sweat glistening on his skin. He never stopped moving, for which Gilbert was grateful.

Gilbert didn't stop with Richie's nipples. Since Richie seemed to enjoy what Gilbert was doing, Gilbert continued touching him. He rubbed his palms down Richie's stomach but stopped before touching his cock. Instead of doing that, he moved both his hands behind Richie, grabbing his ass. Richie seemed to enjoy that, because he slammed down harder than he had before. Gilbert could feel he was about to come, but he wanted Richie to do so before him. In this situation, Richie was more important than Gilbert.

So Gilbert grabbed one of Richie's thighs with one hand and his cock with the other. Richie leaned back, exposing his body and offering it to Gilbert. Gilbert jacked him off, unable to look away. Richie was always beautiful, but right now? He was everything Gilbert had ever wanted and had never allowed himself to hope for. He was everything, period.

Richie threw his head back and moaned loudly. His cock jerked in Gilbert's hand, and he came, splattering Gilbert and himself with cum. His ass contracted around Gilbert, and since he didn't stop moving, the drag and pull on Gilbert's cock did it. Gilbert came, too, squeezing his eyes shut because it was too much.

He'd never come inside anyone like this. The few times he'd topped, he'd always worn a condom. This was incredibly different, yet, at the same time, it wasn't.

Richie slumped on top of Gilbert. He didn't move after that, and while he wasn't that much bigger than Gilbert, he was heavy. Gilbert tried to push him off, but Richie wouldn't bulge.

"I'm dead," he murmured.

Gilbert laughed. Both he and Richie shook with the movement, which made Richie look up.

"I don't want a moving pillow," he complained.

"Then maybe you should move." Gilbert took a chance and poked his fingers into Richie's side.

Richie yelped and rolled off Gilbert. Gilbert breathed more easily, but, as corny as it sounded, he didn't want Richie to move too far away. Thankfully, Richie seemed to want the same thing, and he snuggled against Gilbert's side.

Once again, Gilbert felt odd. Usually, he was the one who snuggled against his boyfriends, not the other way around. Everything seemed to be different with Richie, but Gilbert didn't mind. If anything, he quite enjoyed it.

"Thank you," Richie whispered.

"Are you thanking me for sex?"

Richie snorted. "No. I'm thanking you for giving me what I needed."

"To me, it looked like you *took* what you needed."

"But you could have said no. You could have pushed me away or insisted on something different. Instead, you let me do what I wanted."

Because he'd obviously needed it. Gilbert had wanted to give him what he needed, so that was what he'd done. Things would change in time, but he was more than happy to continue like this for now.

Richie sighed heavily and pressed even closer, although Gilbert hadn't realized it was possible. "We're doing that again, aren't we?" Richie asked.

"If you want to, sure."

"I do." Richie paused. "Maybe not now, because I'm beat, but eventually."

Thankfully, they both had the day off, so it wouldn't be a problem. They could stay in bed all the time they wanted.

"Are you sure you want me to move in with you?" Richie

asked.

"I am. Have you changed your mind?"

Richie propped himself up on an elbow to look down at Gilbert. "I haven't. I'm a bit hesitant, but it's only because of what happened with Francis, not because I don't want it."

"Good. But I think it's important we find a house with enough room that you can have your own space if you need it."

Richie smiled. "And for children."

Gilbert's mouth went dry. They knew they'd be together in the future, but they hadn't yet talked about it apart from today, and they certainly hadn't mentioned children. "You want kids?"

"Don't you?"

Maybe while naked in bed wasn't the best moment to do this, but then, why not? "Eventually. I feel a bit young to have children right now, although Laurie's doing a good job of it."

"I don't think I'm ready for children just yet," Richie said. "I have a lot of work to do on myself before I can dedicate my life to someone else."

"Both of us are still young anyway. But we could get a dog?"

Richie's smile widened. "Can we? Is that something you want?"

"The only reason I don't have one right now is that it wouldn't be fair to the dog, not with my apartment being so small. But yes, I do want a dog."

"Then, as soon as we move into our house, we'll get one."

Gilbert couldn't stop himself from smiling. He felt like he never could stop when he was with Richie, and while that wasn't the case, Richie did make Gilbert happier than he ever remembered being. Whether it was because they were mates or because they were in love, Gilbert didn't know. He didn't care, either.

He dragged his fingertips down Richie's waist. "So, a dog. How about cats?"

Richie wrinkled his nose. "I suppose it depends on the cat. I like some of them, but some are too bitchy for me."

"Then we'll have to go to the shelter together to choose one."

"I can't wait."

Gilbert couldn't, either. Neither of them was going anywhere right now, though, so he pulled Richie closer to kiss him. That was the one thing he'd missed while they were having sex. He understood the need for Richie to be in control, but the position hadn't allowed for them to kiss. Now, he could, and he was going to take advantage of it.

Richie certainly didn't seem to mind, and he fell against Gilbert, kissing him back. Gilbert's cock was hardening again, and Richie made a pleased sound in the back of his throat when he found out.

Gilbert relaxed. They had their entire future in front of them, waiting for them, and he couldn't wait to explore it.

CHAPTER SEVEN

R ichie pushed one of the plates closer to the center of the table. He cocked his head, trying to see if it was where it was supposed to be.

An arm wrapped around his waist and pulled him away. "Everything looks perfect. You don't have to worry," Gilbert murmured.

But Richie was a worrier at heart. That hadn't changed, even though he and Gilbert had been together for almost a year now. Gilbert didn't seem to mind, and he was great at pulling Richie away from his thoughts and obsessions.

Which was exactly what he was doing right now.

It had taken them a while to find the perfect house and even longer to renovate it. Thankfully, Richie's family had helped, and now, the house was beautiful. It reflected both Richie's and Gilbert's personalities, which was what Richie had wanted.

And tonight, they were hosting their first family dinner.

That was why Richie was nervous, even though he shouldn't be. His family already knew the house, and they loved it as much as Richie and Gilbert did. They'd been there countless times, helping to paint the walls, put together the kitchen, and move furniture. Still, this was the first official family dinner Richie and Gilbert had in their home, and it was important to Richie.

Gilbert kissed Richie's cheek. "Can I do anything to distract you?" he whispered.

Richie knew what Gilbert could do, but someone knocked

on the front door before he could say so. Gilbert sighed while Richie laughed and pushed away from him. He changed his mind, leaning toward Gilbert again to kiss him on the lips.

"Hold that thought for tonight," he murmured.

Then he looked away from Gilbert and went to the front door.

He flung it open, expecting his family, but surprised to see Jack and Andy on his porch. Usually, they were late.

Richie made a show of looking around. "Where is everyone else?"

Jack pushed past him. "How should I know?"

"Usually, you only arrive when all the work is done. Is there something wrong? Are you ill?"

Jack growled and pushed Richie. "We're not ill. We just wanted to spend some time with you. Since your backyard opens on the woods, we thought we could shift and play around."

Richie beamed. He'd taken that into consideration when he and Gilbert had bought the house. He hadn't been able to shift when he lived with Francis because they were in an apartment. Besides, Francis hadn't wanted him to. He'd always said he didn't like birds and that swans were bitchy. Some were, but Richie had always known that wasn't Francis's real problem.

But he didn't care about his ex's problems. He didn't care about his ex, either.

"Everyone else is going to be here soon," he said.

"So? They can shift and play with us," Jack answered. He moved toward the back of the house, stopping to say hello to Gilbert. "I'm stealing your man for a bit," he declared.

"As long as you bring him back in one piece, feel free."

"Are you sure?" Richie asked when he reached Gilbert. "The others will be arriving soon."

"And I'll either send them outside with the three of you or

put them to work here. Go, have fun with your brothers. I'm not going anywhere."

And Richie finally believed that. It had taken him a while, and he'd been working with a therapist. It hadn't been easy to accept that in instances when Richie believed he wasn't good enough and Gilbert would eventually realize that, it was Francis speaking. Francis had pushed him down because he'd been afraid to lose him and the control that he had over him, so he'd made sure he believed he wasn't good enough.

But he'd failed. Richie was free, and he was happier than he'd ever thought he could be. The three years he'd spent with Francis had been the darkest point of his life, but they were behind him now. He had everything he could ever want—a beautiful home, a loving mate, a great family. He was still working with Sean, and he thought he would continue doing so because he enjoyed it. He and Richie still had to get a dog, since they'd waited until the house was finished to do so. Tomorrow, they were going to the shelter, and they'd come home as three.

Then, somewhere down the line, they'd add kids to their family. Just thinking about it made Richie's eyes prickle. He'd been lucky, being able to get away from Francis, but not only that. He was strong, and he had to remember that.

"Coming?" Jack called out.

Richie hurried after him and Andy. They were already naked, and Jack shifted as soon as Richie joined them. Andy winked at Richie and followed their brother's example, and Richie stopped hesitating and worrying. He took off his clothes, dumping them onto the bench he and Gilbert had bought for that reason, then he let his swan come out.

He opened his wings and shook them. Since he'd come back home, he'd shifted more often than he had over the entire three years with Francis, so it wasn't as new as it had been in the beginning. It still felt freeing, though, and Richie honked in pleasure. A giggle answered him, and he turned to see that Laurie, Alexis, and Melissa had arrived. Melissa was pulling on her t-shirt, clearly wanting it off so she could shift. She'd started shifting a few months ago, and she loved it. It made Laurie and Alexis's life more complicated. But both of them were shifters, and they had help from their families.

Laurie huffed. "You know how long it took me to choose those clothes and put them on her?" he said.

Richie honked.

Laurie sighed when Melissa almost threw herself out of his arms. "Fine. I'll remember this, though."

He would, but the threat was empty. He loved his daughter, and he would never do anything to hurt her.

He and Alexis helped Melissa out of her clothes. She was barely naked when she shifted, and she ended up with a sock still on her now webbed foot. She shook it to get the sock off, but she wasn't great at balance yet, whether in her human form or her swan form. She tilted forward, honked in dismay, and fell.

Richie rushed to her. He rubbed his beak against hers, then helped her to her feet.

"Keep an eye on her, will you," Laurie said.

Richie nodded. Melissa waddled after him, her gray fluff all over the place. It would take her a while to gain the black feathers Richie and his brothers shared, but she would, eventually. In the meantime, she was the cutest thing Richie had ever seen.

Richie, Jack, and Andy kept close to Melissa and made her play. By the time they were done and ready to eat, the rest of the family had arrived. They'd gathered on the porch, laughing and talking, and Gilbert looked at home between them.

He was. Gilbert's father might not want him in his life, but Richie's family did. They'd adopted him before he even met Richie, but now that they were together, he would never have to leave them behind. Richie knew how happy that made him, and it made Richie happy, too.

During the three years with Francis, he'd thought he'd lost everything. Maybe he had, for a bit. He'd left, though, and he'd gotten everything back, and more. He had his family, a home, and Gilbert.

Everything he needed.

ABOUT THE AUTHOR

Catherine is the creator of several series, most of them paranormal, including the Whitedell Pride Series and the Gillham Pack Series. While she graduated in translation, she decided to go the writer's way because it was more fun to create her own stories and characters.

She's been living in Italy for more than twenty years, but she's a daughter of the North—Belgium to be precise—and she misses it so much that she's already planning to move back.

She loves pizza—probably too much—her son, her pets, and of course, books. She sneaks some reading time into her schedule every time she has five minutes free from writing, demands from her various pets and son, and lastly, housework.

Connect with her:

lievens.catherine@gmail.com
BookBub: https://www.bookbub.com/authors/catherine-lievens
Website: https://authorcatherinelievens.com/
Facebook: https://www.facebook.com/catherine.lievens.9
Facebook Group: https://www.facebook.com/groups/411788002341528/
Twitter: https://twitter.com/authorCLievens
Newsletter: http://eepurl.com/c-uvKn

www.ingramcontent.com/pod-product-compliance
Lightning Source LLC
Chambersburg PA
CBHW070755120626
46557CB00002B/605